UNBEARABLE THINGS

Copyright © 2021 by Van Hawkins

Library of Congress Control Number: 2021905386
ISBN: 978-0-9863992-5-1

UNBEARABLE THINGS

A NOVEL BY
VAN HAWKINS

Writers Bloc
Jonesboro, Arkansas

ALSO BY VAN HAWKINS

Hampton and Newport News
A look at two historic Virginia towns, 1975

Dorothy and the Shipbuilders of Newport News
The story of an iconic American shipyard, 1976

The Historic Triangle
How Jamestown, Williamsburg, and Yorktown
made American history, 1980

Plowing New Ground
The Southern Tenant Farmers Union and its place
in Delta history, 2007

Duty Bound
The Hyatt brothers and Confederates
of the Third Arkansas Infantry Regiment, 2011

Horizons
A novel about growing up in a small southern town
in the 1950s and 1960s, 2012

Smoke Up the River
Steamboats and the Arkansas Delta, *2016*

Moaning Low: From Slavery to Peonage
Involuntary servitude in the Arkansas Delta, 2019

A New Deal in Dyess:
The Depression Era Agricultural Resettlement Colony
in Arkansas, 2020

The Colonel's Clay
A novel about a boy who apprentices with a legendary
Mississippi River boat gambler, 2020

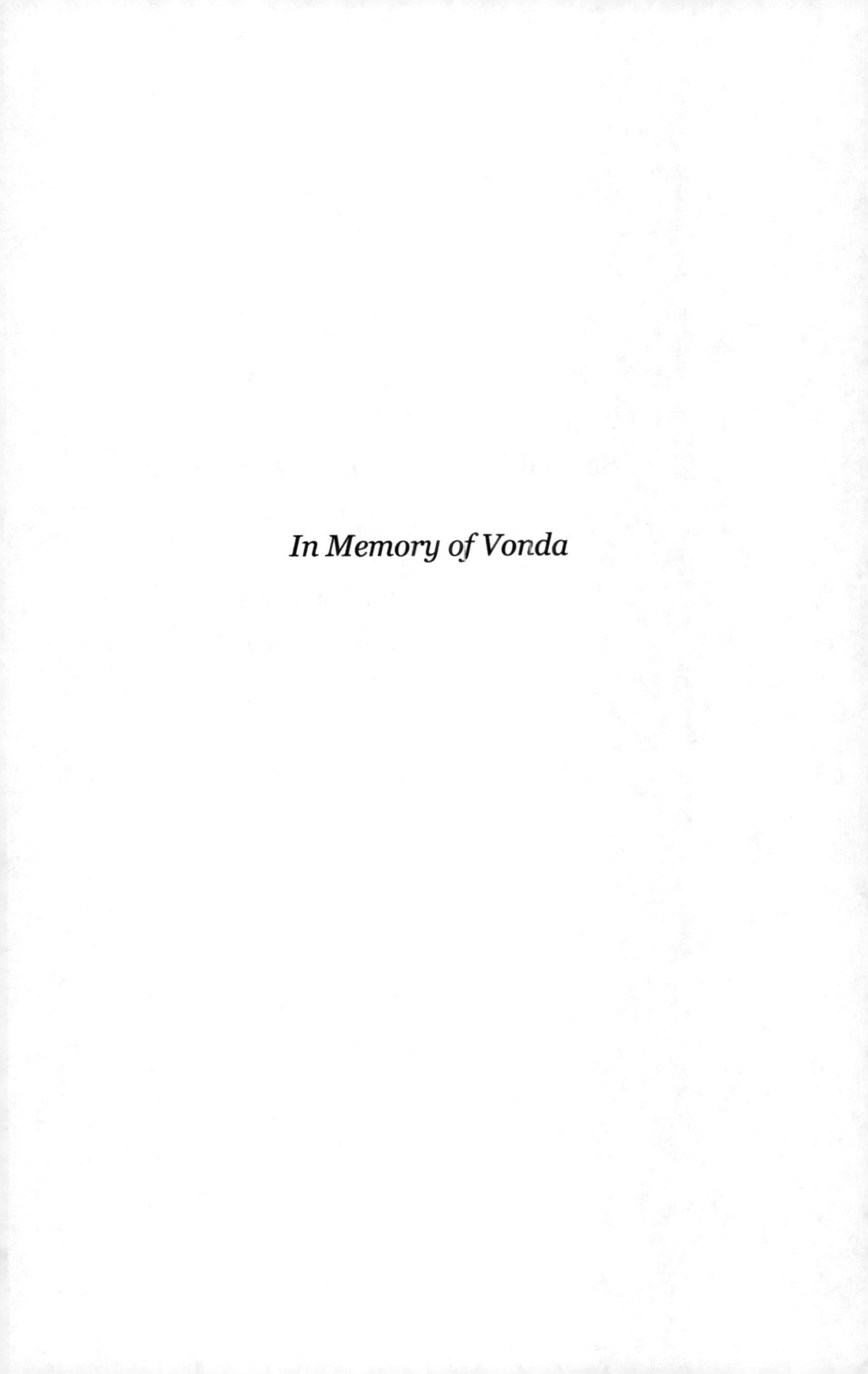

In Memory of Vonda

Some things you must always be
unable to bear.

--William Faulkner

Intruder in the Dust

PART ONE

1

In Norfolk, Virginia, that night a bullet sped through Harold Booker's brain, and he died before his head hit the steering wheel. The window on a nearby car scrolled up after a pistol with a silencer disappeared along with the hand that held it. The driver, Edward Lee, swung out of the strip club parking lot and headed for Virginia Beach. As the rented Ford pulled away, two parking places down a young Marine in a black pickup saw it all, shook his head, and decided that it was not a dream. Shortly thereafter, on a pay phone at a gas station on Witchduck Road, Lee called his handler, known as the Deacon. "The target is down," the killer said.

"Very well then. Finish this business."

Lee hung up and for a moment watched headlights shooting along the expressway like tracers out of a Huey gunship. Later, while the assassin sat at a bar sipping beer, his mind dialed out the jukebox music and crowd noise and replaced them with memories from another time and place. He shooed away the first two women who approached, so others decided not to waste their time unless he became noticeably drunk, which would not happen. One of the women appeared to be Latin American, and that steered Lee's memory to his first kill in Nicaragua. It was a clean double tap that dropped the Cuban mercenary into a rut of muddy water on a rainy day.

As Lee nursed his beer in the Virginia Beach club, Norfolk police detectives Ronnie Boyle and Walter McNabb arrived at the strip club parking lot after a call for help from the bar. Light illuminated the grimy concrete from a flashy sign on the building that read, "Oar House. Come Inside." An additional neon attraction accompanied the offer, a sparsely dressed woman holding a large wooden oar between her legs. Boyle and Mac left their car lights on and went over to look at the body. Being the senior detective, Mac looked first through the open door. The victim had fallen forward with what remained of his head resting on the steering wheel and some of his brains spread out on the fake wood dash. "Single head shot from a distance," Mac said as he reached into the victim's dress-blue uniform pocket and pulled out a wallet with the dead sailor's driver's license. "Name is Harold Booker."

The older cop made room for Boyle to form his own conclusions. The younger detective eased his middle-weight boxer torso into the car and observed what remained of Booker. Following a brief visual examination Boyle turned to the dozen or so gawkers standing nearby and asked, "Who called in the report?"

A bouncer wearing a Grateful Dead t-shirt answered. "A Marine in the parking lot ran inside and told the bartender, and he called the police."

"Did any of you see anything?" Boyle asked the crowd in general, but no one answered. "Where is the Marine now?" Boyle asked the bouncer.

"He's in the bar with a double Black Jack and a Bud chaser."

"Great," Boyle said to Mac. "He'll be too shit-faced to give us anything." Though less experienced than Mac, Boyle caught the case. This was fortunate since most of the day Mac had been drinking gin out of a pint bottle stowed in the glove compartment of a Chevrolet Impala assigned to the detectives. Boyle took charge of the crime scene and signaled to Mac that he would focus on the witness while Mac handled forensics. Before entering the club Boyle directed another question toward the crowd. "Do any of you know the victim?" Again, nothing but silence and shuffling feet.

"All of you stay clear of the car," Mac told the gawkers. "The forensic team is on the way." After that he headed to his car for another swig of gin.

The bouncer ushered Boyle into a large room now well lit and empty, except for a bartender and Marine in fatigues at the bar pondering an almost empty glass. Ceiling lights illuminated a dim reality. What appeared to be spots of spilled beer and vomit dappled parts of the dark tile floor. The corporal looked up woefully at the detective. "I'm totally screwed."

Boyle pulled out his small notebook. "What's your name?"

"Jake Pollard."

"So you shot the guy, and we got you. Is that why you're totally screwed?"

"No. I didn't shoot the guy. I got duty tonight. It was slow, so gunny cut me some slack to go home and be with my wife. She's knocked up and due any day. I only stopped for a couple, but I got sleepy and decided to catch a few in my truck before I drove home. Was just gonna nap for a few minutes, but when I woke up it was a lot later." He sighed, leaning his head on coupled hands. "Ain't no way this is gonna go right with gunny. I wish that dude had shot me instead."

A former Marine, Boyle knew that the man's gunnery sergeant would torment the corporal in every way possible, and in the Corps there were a lot of possibilities. The detective decided to use this as leverage. "How about you help me, and I help you."

"Whatever."

"Where are you stationed?"

"Little Creek."

"Did you know the victim?"

"No."

"Have you fired a weapon recently?"

"No."

"Are you willing to come down to the station and let us test you for gun powder residue?"

"Sure," the Marine responded without realizing that he had just graduated from potential suspect to certain witness.

Boyle moved on. "Tell me what you saw." The detective carefully watched Pollard's facial expressions and body language as he told his story, but interrupted when the Marine described a gun with a silencer extending from the car's open window.   "No way was there a silencer on that weapon. Not in that parking lot."

The witness bristled. "I know what a silencer looks like. I'm recon, and every man on my team has a Glock with a silencer hidden in his kit."

"Maybe you were having a recon flashback."

"I just woke up, but I was up. I saw the silencer. Looked like it was on a Beretta. I couldn't see the shooter. It was too dark in the car. My window was up, and it's tinted. That probably saved my life. He couldn't see me."

"Not enough light to see the shooter, but enough to ID a weapon?"

"The weapon came out of the car window for a few seconds. The shooter didn't. It had a silencer. I'm sure. You want the first three numbers of his license plate or not?"

"Sure."

Pollard gave him the first three plate numbers and a brief description of the Ford, either a light gray or tan. The detective took it all down in his notebook. "You never saw the victim before. That's what you're telling me. I'm not gonna find out from somebody else that you knew the guy and got into a beef about some lap dancer."

"No. I didn't know the guy."

Boyle decided to drop that line of questioning, and the interrogation stopped. He knew his assumption that one drunk shot another drunk over a bar squeeze no longer worked. He also knew that what at first looked like a simple case may have become a time-consuming investigation, and his trip to the Oar House had taken a turn for the worse.

Though First Class Electrician Harold Booker's day ended unexpectedly, it began according to plan. Booker casually saluted an ensign hanging listlessly on the stern mast as he walked up the gangplank onto the quarterdeck of a guided missile destroyer that morning. Chief Boatswain's Mate Pete Gonzales, officer of the deck that morning, welcomed Booker aboard. "When do I get the $100 you owe me?"

"Today."

"Today works for me. I thought we might get a game going tonight."

"Can't. I'm meeting somebody. I'll get with you later."

Booker entered the stern hatch and began his forward march toward operations compartment sleeping quarters where his bunk and locker were located. He mumbled hello to several passing shipmates as he threaded his way through the passage and down a steel ladder into the compartment.

Filled with rows of bunks two deep, the space was empty except for a couple of slackers hurrying to finish dressing so they wouldn't miss muster and go on report. Identical gray blankets, all tucked in tight the Navy way, covered each bunk mattress. Booker twisted his combination lock until it clicked open. Not required to muster, he took his time changing into dungarees for the day's work. Just as Booker started to take out a toolbox stored in his locker a tall signalman named Norman Portman descended the ladder and walked over.

"You hear the news?" he asked Booker.

"What?"

"Washington made chief."

"I didn't know he was up for chief."

"Yeah. Course, being black, you know he got a bump."

"How did you do?" Booker asked while gathering stuff from his locker.

"Hit quota again. Did you apply?"

"No."

"You just give up?"

"Yeah. Don't care anymore."

"If I had your money I wouldn't care either."

Booker removed the tool box from his locker and spun the lock shut. He yanked on the locker door to make sure it was secure and joined Portman for a climb up the steel ladder to the destroyer's main deck. Booker stopped for a cup of strong black coffee on the mess deck where a few sailors were finishing breakfast. He spotted another electrician who waved Booker over to his table.

"You seen the chief yet?" Jarvis Harvey asked.

"No, I just came onboard. Why?"

"Skipper told chief that something is wrong with an overhead light in the wardroom. It must of gone out last night. Anyhow, he wants it squared away first thing. Chief told the skipper he'd get you on it."

"Is the work order ready?"

"Yeah. Lonnie typed one up."

Booker walked away, maneuvering between rows of heavy metal tables bolted to the gray deck. He climbed down a steel ladder into a passageway that led to the electrical shack as an E3 finished typing another work order. The typist looked up as Booker walked in.

"Man am I glad to see you. Have you seen the chief?" the typist asked.

"No, he's probably in the coffee mess. Have you got the wardroom work order?"

"Yeah," the sailor replied as he handed the paperwork to Booker.

"The overhead light won't work. Is that all that's wrong?"

"I guess. That's all the skipper told the chief. The chief told him you'd get on it first thing."

"The wardroom should be cleared out by now," Booker said. "Tell the chief if he comes in that I'm on it."

"Okay."

Booker's walk to the wardroom was the longest of his life. When he initially agreed to do the job, Booker had been calm, but he became increasingly nervous as the deadline approached. He had considered the event's consequences, which gave him some satisfaction, but the money mattered more than anything else. He would be rich, at least by his standards. Lee knew this when he hired Booker.

As the electrician carried his toolbox the last few feet into the wardroom he appeared nonchalant. Only a Filipino steward remained, and he had just finished clearing the last tray of dirty dishes from a massive oak table. "You done?" Booker asked the steward.

"Just now," the waiter said while heading toward a hatch into the officer galley.

"Tell the boys the wardroom is closed until I get this overhead wiring checked."

"Okay."

Booker locked the galley hatch and one that opened into the passageway. With the space's only two entries secured, he took a Phillips screwdriver from his kit and quickly removed four screws that held one of the air vent covers high on a bulkhead near the overhead. Booker opened his tool box and withdrew five pounds of C4, an electric blasting cap, a six-volt battery, and a receiver. He placed the blasting cap in the C4, wired the cap to the receiver, attached the receiver to the battery, and set the frequency. Booker inserted the bomb deep into the vent opening, well out of sight should someone take off the slatted cover and look inside. He replaced the cover and looked at his watch. Less than five minutes had passed. Booker then removed the base plate from an overhead light above the large table and secured wiring he had loosened the night before. When the electrician walked out of the wardroom he marveled that such simple steps taken in a brief span of time could cause such enormous harm to the U. S. Congress and Navy, two organizations he despised.

Booker returned to the electricity shack where the chief was scanning the day's work orders. "What about the wardroom. You figure out what's wrong up there?" the chief asked.

"Just a loose wire."

"What caused that?"

"Don't know. Maybe one of the security men monkeyed with the light. Anyhow, it's squared away."

"I'm damn glad those security people finished yesterday. It chaps my ass that they think they got to inspect our ship, like we can't take care of our own security."

Booker nodded in agreement and moved on to the next step in his plan. "I got to go ashore to the NOB clinic. Got a problem."

"Why don't you go to sickbay?"

"I want a real doctor to look at me, not Chief Savoy. I'm passing some blood. I may need to check in for tests."

"Okay. Use liberty until you get it taken care of. I'll prepare a medical chit and leave the dates open."

"Thanks," Booker replied. This excuse would allow him time to deliver a transmitter to his handler and collect the remaining money owed him. It also set up his story about taking a few days off before the explosion. If everything went as planned, he would never hear liberty call again.

2

After Doc Hardesty stepped out of the shower the next morning and looked at his silhouette in the mirror, he saw a receding hairline and expanding waistline. "Damn!" he said to himself. Doc looked away, irritated and disgusted. "Damn!" he said again, moving closer to the sink as he prepared to shave. Doc worried that in a few years he would become a fat, bald alcoholic with lung cancer if he didn't change his ways. Doc vowed to stop smoking two packs of cigarettes a day, but decided to begin withdrawal the following week. He considered getting fat not his fault. It was unavoidable due to DNA from his mother. His expanding waistline had nothing to do with spending too much time on a bar stool at the Recovery Room, his favorite tavern.

As Doc lathered up to shave, he heard Karen snoring softly in the bedroom. His small rent house sat on

Willoughby Spit, a sliver of land that stretched from Norfolk to a point where the James River spilled into Chesapeake Bay. He enjoyed evenings with Karen when she stayed over because she was attractive and quiet, two qualities Doc appreciated. Unfortunately, Karen wanted more from him. The negotiation began when she volunteered to do his laundry with hers since she had to do hers anyhow. Next came housework and cooking. Recently Karen had been lamenting about difficulties making her apartment rent on a paltry waitress salary. But what else could she do? She had no place else to stay.

Doc stopped shaving and stared hard into the mirror. I'll miss her, he thought, but Karen was disturbing the equilibrium. So he would have to find a pliable alternative, another waitress to become his caregiver. He chose waitresses because they usually had low maintenance costs. "El memento del verdad," he said to himself, wondering if the line came from Pancho Villa or a bandit in that Bogart movie about gold mining. He couldn't decide which.

Doc pulled his overworked and underserviced black Datsun Z into the *Norfolk Gazette* parking lot a bit late, but managed to run though most of the police reports by the time the city editor reached his desk among the long rows of reporter stations throughout the newsroom. "Do you have anything?" the editor asked Doc.

"A strip club murder, two nickel and dime holdups, and a barroom brawl at the Acey Deucy between sailors and Marines. Just a normal night on the town."

"Was the murder victim a politician?" Carter Stone asked.

"No, a sailor."

"Too bad, another lost opportunity."

Doc liked Stone's sense of humor, but he found his editor's appearance irritating. Stone excelled as a pole vaulter at Columbia University and earned a journalism degree there. He had a pale complexion and slim muscular build with long, straight black hair and an aquiline nose. Stone rose early some mornings to surf at Virginia Beach, which enhanced his image. That morning Stone quickly settled on the murder. Doc pushed for good play on page one of the city section below the fold, but Stone hesitated for a moment before giving in.

"Okay. Front below the fold, but one column, six inches, no jump. Nothing more until you get enough for a follow-up."

Stone moved to the next desk, where his military reporter had a story about black congressmen scheduled to visit Norfolk for a one-day ride on a guided missile destroyer.

Doc then called Boyle to find out more about the murder. "Tell me about the homicide. Have you identified the victim?"

"Yeah, I caught it. We went to the sailor's house last night and told his wife. Her mind is out there where the buses don't run. The sailor was a lifer named Harold Booker, grew up in Tennessee, a good ol' boy."

"Why do you say that?"

"His record collection. A rack full of outlaw country. His life apparently revolved around bad music, poker, and airplanes, at least according to his wife and buddies."

"What kind of planes?"

"Small hobby planes. People fly them in parks using transmitters and receivers. One of our patrolmen once loaned me his to show my kids. The things are interesting. You control them with the transmitter."

After Boyle laid out the facts Doc asked, "So what drunk at the Oar House killed him?" Several heartbeats passed without a reply. "Come on Ronnie, don't short me. Remember, I'm your buddy."

"So you say. You have to sit on this until I tell you different. You break your word and I'll cut off your nuts and feed 'em to squirrels."

"You convinced me."

"We found several interesting items when our people tossed the car--a bag of coke and too much cash for a sailor. Mac and I talked to Chief Gonzales on the destroyer early this morning. He said Booker had been flashing a gangster roll and supposedly won it gambling. But Gonzales said Booker was a terrible poker player. Lost most of the time. The really strange thing is that a dependable eyewitness got a look at the gun and said the shooter used a silencer."

"A silencer. Are you sure?"

"As sure as we're ever gonna be."

"What is this about?" Doc asked, more to himself than Boyle. "Give me what else you got on it."

Boyle continued and closed by saying, "That's it so far, and you better sit on it."

"I will, but this may be part of a large drug deal that went upside down."

"Call it what you want, but if I were you I'd bird dog this one."

Doc laid down the receiver and reviewed his notes. An E6 electrician aboard a guided missile destroyer is shot in a strip joint parking lot by a person with a silencer. The killer apparently did not see a weary Marine asleep in his truck who got part of the car tag as the killer drove away. The cops found coke and a lot of cash in the victim's car. It looked like a busted drug meet, but most local drug-related crime involved gangbangers killing everybody in the room but the guy they were shooting at. The Marine's gunnery sergeant assured Boyle that the police could believe what Pollard said about the shooting. Doc handed the city desk a brief story since the important stuff had to be withheld until Boyle went on the record with it.

The cop knew that Doc would keep his word. The reporter always did no matter how important the story. They trusted each other, at least up to the point where self-interest ended. Both had served with the Marines, though Doc did so as a Navy medic. Boyle had become a valuable source not to be burned. Though a good cop, he owed Doc and sometimes violated department regulations by leaking information on background to the reporter.

The detective's wife had an alcohol problem. She drank too much of it. The previous year a disgruntled patrolman called Doc claiming that Boyle had fixed a drunk driving ticket for his wife. When Doc confronted Boyle about the allegation the detective didn't blink. He admitted his wife's drinking problem and told Doc she had gone through rehab, joined AA, and been sober for three months. But the reporter should do what he thought right given these circumstances.

Doc chose to spike the story and never regretted his decision. They developed a friendship of sorts, though neither newspaper reporters nor cops ever have real friends. Their bond strengthened when the detective checked with several Marines that Doc served with in Vietnam. Doc had earned their respect, and in the Corps respect did not come on the cheap. The Marines said that when a man fell, Doc found a way to him, regardless of the risk. Unfortunately, Doc's experiences led to a cynicism that made him unfit for any profession other than a newspaper reporter.

Doc's notes held another bit of interesting information. NCIS had become involved in the case. He turned to Annie Clausen, a military reporter at the next desk. Clausen had red curly hair and a temper to match. He raised his voice to be heard above the clattering IBM Selectrics that engulfed the newsroom at deadline. "Clausen, anything new in the military drug war?"

She shouted back impatiently. "Nothing new. Half the fleet are alcoholics, the other half junkies."

"Can you give me something on a DDG?"

"Probably, why?"

"One of the crew got himself shot in a strip club parking lot last night."

"The Navy is having a bad week."

"How so?"

"Three days ago a sailor at Yorktown Naval Weapons Station killed himself."

Since Doc's police beat did not cover Yorktown he disregarded that news. His next move took Doc into the newspaper's clip files pertaining to recent drug-related military stories. The search kept him there until Clausen walked up. "That ship is squeaky clean. The new skipper is black. He's Academy and apparently a hard ass. Several members of the congressional black caucus are scheduled to go aboard for a 12-hour cruise. Why do you want to know?"

"I'm doing a backgrounder on military drug use."

"You're lying. Don't ask for anything else while you're hoarding."

"Clausen you always believe the worst of people. But I'll forgive the insult and buy you a drink at the Recovery Room after work."

"Waste of time, Doc. I'm not that thirsty. Never will be. What's wrong, is your latest waitress bunny out of town? Must be at a Mensa conference."

Despite this failure Doc wanted to achieve one thing for certain that morning. He planned to meet Karen at home for lunch since she called in sick to spend a day on the beach. Doc decided to tell her the time had come for both of them to move on. He drove home dreading the confrontation. After summoning his courage he walked into the kitchen. While stirring their seafood chowder, one of his favorite dishes, Karen wore a black bikini. Doc studied her for a moment and decided to postpone the expulsion in order to spare her feelings.

3

The man who shot Booker also made an abrupt change of plans the next morning. When Lee walked out of a motel office in Virginia Beach after paying his bill with cash, he saw two police cruisers at the other end of the parking lot by his rental car. As one patrolman peered through its window the other called in the location of a car with the partially identified license plate and general description given them.

Momentarily taken aback and incredulous that his car may have been connected to the shooting, Lee quickly adjusted. Since he had carefully wiped down the car and room, his identity could not be ascertained by fingerprints. Lee toted his one piece of luggage down the street to catch a cab and analyze every step in his movements to determine what had gone wrong and why.

Doc got bad news when he walked into the partially deserted newsroom on Saturday. He learned that Boyle was unavailable. Another disappointment came when Karen called. "Don't forget that you agreed to take me to the Recovery Room tonight and get a beer with some of my friends."

"Karen, I forgot about it. I'm sorry. I can't make it."

"You promised, and it's Brenda's birthday. You've always got some excuse. Now you promised, and this is important to me."

After her rant Doc folded. "Okay, I'll go."

Two of Karen's waitress buddies and their uninteresting boyfriends joined them, and Doc drank too much beer to decline their offer to go bowling. At the bowling alley the women stuffed quarters into a jukebox playing country songs, and Doc drank more beer to drown out the music. Karen noted the binge and confronted him at the bar. "Honey, is something wrong?"

"Yeah, that music is nauseating." After that comment Karen suggested they go home. The trip turned out to be a short one. They had hardly pulled out of the parking lot when a Norfolk patrolman pulled them over. The cop didn't buy his story about having only two glasses of sherry at a family reunion honoring his parents' 50-year wedding anniversary. So Doc went to jail.

He had interesting company in the large holding cell --
two winos who hadn't bathed in years and a young man who
sat in a corner singing Elvis Presley's greatest hits. Another
man, severely beaten, caressed the cold concrete floor and
moaned. Doc suppressed his inclination to help the injured
man and bid his time in silence. When a desk sergeant
booked Doc he asked the cop for a favor. "Would you please
call my dear friend Ronnie Boyle and tell him about this
grave injustice?"

About an hour later his clearly irritated dear friend
walked up to the cage and offered his preliminary opinion:
"You fucking moron."

By that point in his adventure Doc had sobered up
somewhat. "I agree, but I need help and a ride home."

"Come on," Boyle said. "I'll get you out and keep it off
the sheet, but I can't fix it for you. Everybody in the precinct
knows about it, and they all hate your guts. You'll have to
work the rest out on your own."

Doc took the deal and ride, and Boyle parked for a few
minutes in the driveway of his cottage in order to share
information. "NCIS took over the Booker case, or so I'm
told. Chief pulled me off it after he called me into his office.
The two guys in there when he told me were supposedly
NCIS."

"Supposedly?"

"Yeah, but their suits were too good for NCIS."

"Okay, I'll dig deeper. I can't work on it tomorrow because I promised Karen I'd take her to Nags Head. She likes the beach down there."

Doc began working on his latest problem on Monday morning. He dialed the private number of Keefer Monroe, the most unprincipled, outrageous, and successful criminal lawyer in Tidewater. Monroe would defend a sociopathic serial killer if the monster's check cleared the bank. Occasionally Doc ran a leak from the lawyer and had some leverage, or so he thought.

Monroe expressed extreme displeasure when the call came in on a separate, must-answer, unlisted line. "What!" he exclaimed.

"It's Doc. I'm in a jam."

"Did you kill somebody in front of witnesses?"

"No."

"Then you're not in a jam. Call me tomorrow."

"I got a DUI."

"So chop a line and forget about it. Do you know what time it is? My office hours are 11 to 1 with an hour off for lunch. You know that."

"I need this taken care of today before word hits the city desk." Doc heard a female voice in the background urging Monroe to hang up and rejoin her.

"Okay, I'll take care of it. Right now I'm in the middle of something."

Later that morning while Doc hammered out a thin follow-up about the Oar House shooting, Lee sat in a Williamsburg café booth having a cup of coffee. Tourists thronged to Colonial Williamsburg, making it excellent cover for a face to get lost in a crowd. Lee assumed that law enforcement agencies throughout the area had a description of him provided by the Virginia Beach hotel manager, but he looked different now. Lee had a shaved head, full beard, artificial but perfect, and large black sunglasses. He had another problem. A newspaper story in the *Norfolk Gazette* indicated that the trip he sought to sabotage had been delayed a few days. Black congressmen remained in Washington for a critical vote on a bill expanding laws against discrimination.

This provided more time for someone to discover the explosives, but security agents had already cleared the vessel, which reduced that risk. Lee had concluded that someone saw him drive away from the strip club and identified his car. But he decided not to inform his employers about his stumble because they might shoot lame horses.

While the killer pondered his problem, Doc considered his predicament should the city editor find out that his police reporter spent time in the Norfolk jail drunk tank. But this preoccupation ended when Boyle called. Doc answered, "Hello. This is the fucking moron you busted out of jail. Did you keep my name off the sheet?"

"Yeah. And now that you're sober, are you doing anything about the Booker story? Something strange is going on."

"Well, you're the detective. What have you detected?"

"I got a call from a York County deputy sheriff, a friend of mine, who caught the so-called Yorktown suicide. He's mad because the two good suits have taken over his case too."

"How do you know it's the same two suits?"

"He described them spot on. The Yorktown medical examiner ruled that case a suicide, so I can't see why the good suits are looking at it?"

"Can your friend help us with that question?"

"He said he'd try."

"So what are you supposed to be working on instead of the Booker case?"

"Car jackings in Ghent."

"They pulled you and Mac off Booker to chase car thieves you'll never catch?"

"Yeah. You got it."

"What does Mac have to say about all this?"

"Mac's only regret at this point is he didn't retire the day before Booker's murder."

"So share your thoughts with me."

"It's part instinct and part facts. The shooter is a pro. That's for sure. There has to be someone with serious money behind him. Everything I've found out about Booker goes against him being involved in the drug business or flush with cash he picked up from a poker table. That doesn't track. I wonder if someone planted drugs and money in Booker's car to push the investigation toward a deal that went sideways. We got lucky. No way could the shooter have planned for a sleepy Marine parked nearby with a good eye for details. The crewmen who knew Booker well said he couldn't be dealing because some of them would have known it. They said Booker carried a lot of cash, but didn't win it playing poker. Everybody I've interviewed agrees on those points. Don't let this one fall through the cracks."

"Don't worry, this one is interesting." Doc knew that Boyle had a personal motive for sharing information. The reporter could go places out of bounds to cops because of legal constraints, and Doc went out of bounds often. "Give me what you got on the car thefts so I have something to feed my city editor's ravenous appetite for news." Boyle did, and signed off.

However, car thieves didn't interest Stone. "Where are we on a follow up to that sailor's murder?"

"I'm on it. I'm going totos porcus with it."

"I take it that's Latin, but I have no idea what it means."

"It means whole hog."

The city editor shook his head. "How do you come up with that crap?"

"You forget that I'm the son of a Missouri hog farmer. We all speak Latin."

Stone ignored him and walked to Clausen's desk.

Doc's problems increased that afternoon when Tiny confronted him as the reporter prepared to leave an almost empty newsroom. Weighing about 450 pounds and more than six feet tall, Tiny was probably the largest man in Tidewater and for certain the meanest. He had several business interests, pimping, taking book, and collecting debts for shylocks. He also worked for Monroe. After Tiny ambled over to Doc's desk he immediately came to the point. "I'm here for Keefer's money."

"What money?"

"The money you owe him for fixin' your ticket."

"Did the ticket disappear already?"

"Yeah, you got charged with improper passing. The serious stuff is gone."

"How much do I owe Keefer?"

"A thousand dollars."

Doc threw his head back and almost swallowed his tongue, but not quite. "Are you shittin' me! I don't have a thousand dollars. I've never had a thousand dollars, and I ain't ever gonna have a thousand dollars."

"I don't set Keefer's fees. I just collect the accounts receivable."

"Well, you can do what you got to do because I don't have that kind of money. Actually, right now I don't have any money."

"How much you got on you?"

"You want me to empty my pockets right now?"

"Yeah, right now." After Doc scrounged only twelve dollars in cash and some change Tiny became impatient. "What about checking. How much you got in checking?"

Doc pulled out a checkbook from his back pocket. He opened it, saw the balance of $52.74, and handed it to Tiny, whose attitude darkened even more. "What about CDs. You got any CDs?"

"No. How would I get a CD? You don't understand how the newspaper business works. People who own newspapers get stinking rich. People who work for them stay stinking poor."

Tiny frowned and picked up Doc's telephone. "How do I get an outside line?" Doc told him, and Tiny punched in a number. After an answer, he explained the situation. "This motherfucker ain't got no money, chief." Monroe's accounts receivable director listened and nodded. He hung up before Doc could talk him into handing over the receiver.

"I need to talk to Keefer. I want him to tell me how much my floating his stories is worth. I figure a thousand dollars is about right."

"I'll pass it along, but right now you got to help yourself. Today you're gonna write me a check for $50. Every Friday at five I'm gonna come by for at least another $50. I quit comin' when the chief gets $500. You're gettin' a discount because the chief likes you. Ain't no VIG either, so the number won't bump every week. If I don't get any money some Friday I take the keys to your car and sell that raggedy ass motherfucker to my car jockey cousin. You hear what I'm saying?"

Facing only bad options, Doc took the deal. As he watched Tiny lumber away the reporter took some satisfaction in having his current paycheck in a desk drawer.

That night, with Karen on shift, Doc had the tv to himself. He had popped open a beer and settled in for an episode of *Bonanza* when the phone rang. It was Stone, and he was unhappy. "Why are you not here schmoozing with your colleagues?"

Doc realized that he had forgotten about a Virginia Press Association awards banquet, but he hadn't planned to attend anyhow. "Would you believe I stayed home to research an important story that might win the two of us a Pulitzer Prize?"

"No. I wouldn't believe that. So go to your closet and put on that suit that went out of style in the late 50s and get to the Hilton banquet room."

"Carter, please get me out of it. I'll owe you bigtime."

"Can't. Word is you're receiving a major award, and the M. E. wants you here. I assume that in your acceptance speech you're supposed to mention his leadership role. We haven't begun dinner yet so you have plenty of time. No excuses. Show up."

Doc did, and accepted the highest state prize for investigative reporting about justice system failures to protect a battered woman and her son. During his acceptance remarks Doc exaggerated his managing editor's support in preparing the series.

4

The next morning Doc called Boyle first thing. "Give me something good, Ronnie, I'm depressed."

"It's good or bad depending on your point of view. My Yorktown friend found out that the good suits have requested an inventory of explosives at Yorktown Naval Weapons Station. It seems there may be some missing, and the alleged suicide may have had access to it."

"What kind of explosives?"

"Don't know. I asked him that. He said he'd try to find out and let me know. He also said he's not buying the suicide. The dead gunner's mate had a wife and three kids. On the morning of the day he supposedly killed himself the sailor made arrangements to take his family to the Eastern Shore this coming weekend. His wife says he was upbeat and happy. His buddies at Yorktown said the same. The weapon was a Beretta. Local cops found it on the floor. His wife said he never owned a pistol, only a shotgun for bird hunting."

"I'll have to talk to my city editor soon if we get deeper into that death. It's not my beat." After a moment's reflection Doc said, "So we now have two probably murdered sailors. One had cash and coke that may have been planted. The other may have stolen powerful explosives. They were probably killed by a high-priced professional. And good suits are scoping both after sidelining everyone else. This could be a big one if I can put it together."

"That's my take away too."

Doc went home late and fell asleep on the couch while watching *Have Gun Will Travel*.

When he checked the paper's first run the next day Doc found on the state page a thinly sourced story by Clausen about the Yorktown case. Authorities were investigating a breach of security at Yorktown Naval Weapons Station, according to her source. Doc turned toward her. "Hey Clausen."

"Whatever help you want the answer is no because You're hoarding." As Doc turned back to his desk Clausen swiveled in his direction. "Wait. I meant to congratulate you after the awards ceremony, but you must have raced out of there after the presentation."

"I did. I'm no good at that kind of stuff. It embarrasses me."

"Why? You earned that award."

"Maybe so, but I feel like it came at the expense of a murdered mother and her son."

"Why did you choose to build the series around them?"

"It started after a police contact showed me the crime scene photos. That stays between us. He'd get fired if it got out. There was blood all over her and the boy. Brenda Coleman had gone to the cops twice after her ex-boyfriend beat her up. She told them the guy said he was going to kill her and the boy if she didn't let him move back into her apartment."

"Did the cops do anything?"

"They picked him up, but he only got a little jail time. A judge gave him an order saying he had to leave her alone. Like a violent sadist is going to pay any attention to a piece of paper. Then he killed them. A lot of her friends and relatives knew the story so I had plenty of sources to work. It really pissed me off that the system let it happen. The cops said they couldn't arrest the guy for saying he was going to kill them. He had to kill them first."

"So they didn't do anything to stop him."

"No. The court didn't stop him either. The guy terrorized her for months. Every miserable day she lived with fear. That's why I unloaded on the cops and judges. I wanted them to take responsibility and admit they failed her. Didn't make me popular with either group. Does that answer your question?"

"It does. So what do you want to know?"

"Have you heard anything from your Yorktown sources about the deaths of your sailor and my sailor being connected?"

"No. What do you know about that?"

"Nothing yet. I'm just trolling. I'll let you know if I find something."

Doc drove home with a series of questions swirling in his head, but no answers. When he walked into the bungalow Doc saw Karen on the couch painting her toenails bright red. "Did you have a good day honey?"

"Way short of wonderful. So your honey is going to light up a joint."

Karen frowned as Doc pulled out a joint bartered from Monroe that he hid in a Bible. "I wish you wouldn't hide drugs in the Bible. I think that's a bad sin, and I'm afraid God is going to punish you and maybe me even though I don't have anything to do with it."

Doc sank into a worn, overstuffed easy chair and started to light the joint, but paused after digesting Karen's remarks. "I keep forgetting that you're a preacher's daughter. But I can say authoritatively, having grown up in a Baptist pew on Sundays, that nowhere does it say in the Sermon on the Mount that you can't hide a joint in the Bible. I don't think Jesus had a problem with it."

"That's not funny."

"I know it's not funny, but it's true."

After that remark she traipsed into the bedroom. Doc watched her go, then took a hit on the weed and tuned in *Wyatt Earp*.

The next morning became more interesting after a phone call from Boyle. "Yorktown security found out that some C4 is unaccounted for. That's the missing explosives. They tossed the sailor's house but found no cash or explosives."

"Does C4 have any use other than blowing things up?"

"Not that I'm aware of."

"So how does that case connect to Booker?"

"Don't know."

"How do we find out about making a bomb with C4 and connecting it to Booker?"

"I know a demolition guy on a D. C. bomb squad. I met him in Nam. He was working black ops. Harry definitely knows what he's doing, but I can't go farther out on this limb. You'll have to handle it. I'll call him first. Harry will trust me when I tell him your phone call is down low."

"Tell him that's a sure thing."

After Boyle provided Harry's home number Doc called that evening. His wife said her husband would not be home until after his shift, so Doc asked for a return call. It came about an hour later.

When Doc identified himself a strong, firm voice responded. "Ronnie told me you have some general questions, and the answers will never come back and bite me."

"That's correct. You can trust me."

"Let's be clear. I don't know you so I don't trust you, but I trust Ronnie."

After laying it all out Doc asked the central question. "So what have I got?"

"Maybe nothing, or maybe something. C4 can make one hell of an explosion, depending on how much is used. The gunner's mate who may or may not have killed himself probably wouldn't know how to construct a bomb, but an E6 electrician probably would. You mentioned airplanes with remote controls. They could trigger one if properly set up. Given that type of explosive someone in the military or ex-military is probably involved."

"What would be the range on something like that?"

"It would depend on the model and whether the system had been enhanced. Wild guess, I would say maybe a hundred yards. A bomb like that can kill somebody or everybody. The problem is evading discovery. You can kill people, even a president, fairly easy. But escaping makes it far more complicated."

"If you were doing it how would you handle that problem?"

"Well, I wouldn't want to be standing in a crowd with a transmitter in my hand or any place with security nearby. I would want to be isolated, some place with easy egress and nearby cover. Listen, you and Ronnie may be in way over your heads. Have you talked to the FBI about any of this?"

"No, but that comes next."

"If I were you I'd move up the next part to right away. You definitely shouldn't sit on this. It's serious stuff."

Harry ended the conversation with that warning, and Doc sensed that the cop didn't want to know more about it. But who could be the target? Doc wondered. He decided to try another avenue.

Sticks was a junkie informant who loved slender bread sticks from a small Italian café at Ward's Corner. He often walked around with several in his pockets. That day Doc found him in the cafeteria of a rundown Norfolk bus station. The stool next to Sticks was empty, probably due to his questionable hygiene, so Doc took it. Sticks wore military fatigues too large for his skinny frame, and after looking at Doc briefly he continued to slurp the bean soup.

"It's your lucky day, Sticks. I'm going to pay for your delicious meal and give you ten dollars."

"That won't buy much," Sticks said, shaking his shaggy head covered by greasy hair.

"I want answers to two questions."

"Okay, give me the ten dollars."

"You give me the answers, and then I give you the ten dollars."

"What are the questions?"

"Who is buying or selling explosives locally? And has a Navy E6 electrician named Booker been involved in the local drug market?"

"Okay, give me the ten dollars."

"Answers first."

Sticks shrugged and focused on the soup.

"So?"

"Give me the ten dollars or go away."

"Are your answers any good?"

"What's good about this world. Name something."

"Well, you got me there." Doc handed the ten to Sticks, who took it with greasy fingers and pushed his green lunch bill toward Doc.

Sticks had two short answers. "An E6 is a lifer, and lifers don't deal drugs. Only young cheese dicks do because they don't know what happens when they start using the stash. I've never heard of explosives on the street. I don't know of anyone who would touch it. Too much risk. A lot of feds would look at it."

Sticks stopped, but Doc pressed ahead. "Can you ask around. Maybe check with Rogue."

"Won't do any good. He'll say the same thing."

Sticks' brother Rogue led an outlaw motorcycle gang called the Thrusters. These large, violent men had their sticky fingers in criminal activities throughout Tidewater. They also knew everything else going on. Doc met Rogue only once, the same night he met Sticks. When Doc looked out his window one evening he saw Sticks attempting to break into his car. Doc walked outside holding a claw hammer, stood behind Sticks, and noticed that the would-be car jacker had the DTs. His hands shook so bad that he couldn't snake his wire around the window glass to pull up the door lock.

When Doc spoke Sticks jumped and dropped the wire. "You have to be the worst car thief I've ever seen."

"Man, I'm sorry, but I need some wheels."

"You can't drive a car in the shape you're in."

"You gonna call the cops?"

"No. Do you know somebody who can come get you?"

"I got a brother."

"Give me his telephone number?"

Sticks pulled out a yellow post-it from his pocket and handed it to Doc. "Call this number and ask for Rogue."

"I take it you're talking about the motorcycle gang leader."

"Yeah. He rolls with the Thrusters."

"Terrific. This story gets better and better."

Doc put Sticks on the porch and went in to call the chop shop where Thrusters broke down stolen vehicles to sell their parts. "Rogue's voice reminded Doc of the sound made when large wheels crush gravel. "Who the fuck are you? What do you want? And how did you get this number?"

"My name is Doc. I live at the end of Willoughby Spit, and your brother gave me the number. I found him trying to boost my car, but he's Jonesing so bad he couldn't drive it."

"Did you call the cops?"

"No. I don't see any point in it. I just want you to come get him. My girlfriend is sleeping in the bedroom, and if she wakes up in this shitshow she'll have a panic attack."

Doc gave Rogue the address, and in about 15 minutes three Harleys roared into his yard. Rogue brought two of his toughest men should the call be an ambush by another gang.

When Sticks walked off the porch Rogue grabbed his shoulders and shook him hard. "What were you doing you dipshit?"

"I was gonna boost it for you to chop and sell the parts for me."

"Shut the fuck up, Sticks. Don't be talkin' my business."

Doc found the scene amusing, but was too nervous to laugh. Rogue turned to him. "So what do you want? You want money?"

"No. I want you to take him to wherever he calls home so he doesn't kill himself and wreck my car in the process."

Rogue turned toward a burly biker. "Strap him on, and let's get out of here." He then looked at Doc. "I owe you a square, but don't ever call that number again."

"Don't worry, I don't plan to."

5

During a long, uneventful weekend Doc made appointments with Booker's wife and Terry Southard, widow of the Yorktown sailor who supposedly committed suicide. On Monday Doc drove to Booker's house in Suffolk, a small brick rancher that needed yardwork, and pulled into the narrow driveway. Connie Booker opened the door, and Doc saw a woman who probably took more drugs than he did. Doc followed her into a small living room and sat down on a sagging couch covered with thick clear plastic that crinkled. When he pulled out his notebook and looked up, Doc noticed that all around the room were pictures of a chihuahua wearing a red bow tie.

The widow noticed his interest. "That's Chico. He got his little heart broke when my husband died. Chico jumped into the dirty laundry hamper in the bathroom and won't come out."

Though amused, Doc maintained a serious demeanor. "I want to talk to you about your husband if you're up to it."

"I told those policemen everything I know."

"Yes, ma'am, but I'm a reporter. We talked about that on the phone."

"Yes, I remember that now."

"How did the two of you meet?"

"We met in Knoxville at a county fair and got married. Harold joined the navy and planned to make it a career, but changed his mind not long ago." After listening to a recitation of irrelevant details, Doc began asking her pointed questions about financial matters.

"Harold always made good money. He would give me a little for odds and ends and paid all the bills. I never complained."

"The guys aboard his ship said he did real well financially. Did he have a second job or inherit some money?"

"Not that I know of, but he did real good."

Do you know of anybody who might want to harm him?"

"I told those policemen that he don't know mean people."

By this point Doc realized the futility of further questions, but he asked one more. "I heard your husband was into remote control planes. Can I see them?"

"Yes. Some are in the garage, but not all of them. I don't know what happened to the others."

He followed her through an entry door into a cramped garage and saw several small planes on a shelf. Doc looked them over briefly and quickly exited after thanking the widow.

On the drive back to Norfolk he complemented himself for setting up the Southard interview for later that afternoon. After the Booker widow he needed a break and a beer.

Terry Southard worked as a dental hygienist in Williamsburg, and after work she met Doc at the door of a two-story old house on a gravel road near Smithfield. She looked fit and forceful.

"Come in," the widow said after opening the door. This time Doc saw several pictures of children. No chihuahuas.

She caught him looking. "Yes, they're all mine. Ages two, six, and eight. They're staying with their grandparents on the Eastern Shore. My in-laws have a home there. I didn't want them in the middle of this mess." She paused and looked away to avoid Doc's eyes. "I don't know what you're looking for here, but I guarantee you Scott did not kill himself. That's what NCIS thinks, or so they say, but they're wrong. I guess that version makes it simple for them. Those people turned this house upside down looking for something, but they wouldn't talk to me about it. They don't care what happened to Scott, but he adored our children and would never kill himself."

Doc opened his notebook and began to write down her quotes. He then asked her for personal background about the Southard lifestyle, hoping to gain information about their financial status. After she finished a lengthy description that revealed no interesting facts, Doc asked, "What do you think happened?"

"I don't know. What version are you pushing?"

The question surprised and irritated him. "I'm not pushing anything. I cover the police beat, and this is part of it. Another sailor died a couple of days after your husband. Did your husband know an E6 electrician named Harold Booker?"

"No. I never heard him mention that name. I read about him in the paper, but that guy was on sea duty out of Norfolk. Scott didn't hang out with sailors except for two or three he worked with. He spent almost all of his spare time with me and the kids. That's one reason I know Scott would never, and I mean never, leave them without a daddy."

Doc placed his notebook on a coffee table to signal that he was going off the record. "Even though this is none of my business, did the two of you have a good marriage?"

"You're right, it's none of your business. But absolutely, we had a good marriage. It wasn't hugs and kisses all the time. Scott was as direct and blunt as I am, so you can appreciate that. But we loved each other and would never do anything to harm one another." She clearly resented the question's inference. "You'll have to forgive my rudeness, but I don't want to talk to you anymore."

Doc stood, prepared to leave, but asked a last question that he disguised with casual comments. "I love the Eastern Shore. I wish I could live over there, but the commute would be too much. Where are your kids staying?"

The widow hesitated, apparently uncomfortable with the question, but answered it anyhow. "My husband's parents bought a house on the eastern edge of Metompkin Inlet."

Doc departed after learning their whereabouts. He wanted to know how to find the house and perhaps elicit useful information from the children and their grandparents. It was a craven and desperate maneuver, but at that point Doc was a desperate man. He made another stop that afternoon, the Oar House parking lot. Faint chalk marks on the concrete remained, and Boyle had given him a diagram of the crime scene showing its critical points. After studying the positions of cars holding the shooter, victim, and witness, Doc realized that it would have been an easy shot for a professional.

Fortunately, Karen had drawn a night shift, so Doc had the bungalow to himself when he arrived home. He popped open a beer and attempted to organize his thoughts until the phone rang. "Did you interview the widows?" Boyle asked.

"Yeah, but as you know, Booker's wife should be in rehab."

"I know. What do you make of the other one? I stayed away from her because of jurisdictional issues."

"I think she's right. I don't think he killed himself. She strikes me as being tough and smart. I doubt she'll answer any more questions, at least from me. That makes two murdered sailors within a couple of days by someone with a serious agenda. My gut tells me they're connected. What do you think?"

"My gut tells me the same thing. Call me if you find out anything else."

The next afternoon Doc found a mom-and-pop real estate office in Hopeton on the Eastern Shore and parked on the asphalt driveway. When he opened the door a bell signaled his entry, and Doc saw an elderly couple eating what appeared to be grilled cheese sandwiches at their cluttered desks. The slender, gray haired man stood and offered his hand. "Hello there, I'm Riley Perkins, and this is my wife Lucille" The elderly woman nodded and took another bite of her sandwich. "What can we do for you?"

"I'm Doc. Not a real doctor. Just a nickname. I'm looking to buy a beach house on Metompkin Inlet."

"Well, you just missed a good one. There are only three livable houses that far out. The other places are fishing lodges privately owned and not fit to live in. The best of the three decent houses sold a couple of weeks ago to a young couple from Yorktown. Lucille and I had it listed."

"I heard about that from a friend. He said the husband's parents bought the house, and they're living there for the time being with their grandkids."

"No, they didn't buy it. Their son and his wife did. We handled the closing for them. We have several other houses listed with oceanfront access we can show you."

"I'm interested," Doc replied to hold the man's attention and goodwill. "Do you mind telling me the price of the one you just sold?"

"No. It's on public record at the courthouse. The owner listed it for $95,000 and got his price. The young couple made a large down payment with cash. You don't hardly see that anymore."

Doc maintained his calm expression, but with difficulty. "I know your sandwich is getting cold. If you give me some brochures and a map to property you have listed I'll drive around and have a look. Then we can talk."

"I sure can." His wife began digging through paperwork on her desk and found a glossy one-sheet. She handed it to Doc, and he noted with relief that it had not been updated since the Metompkin sale. The reporter saw a photo of the house, a large, two-story wood structure on thick stilts for protection against water damage due to exceptionally high tides. The sheet had a map as well. "I appreciate your help."

The old man tried to keep Doc's attention. "I'll be happy to go with you. We have some real good property listed, and I want to show you some. I'd offer you a cheese sandwich, but we ran out of cheese."

Doc smiled. "When I get ready to buy I'll come see you. I promise."

Doc now knew that Scott's widow lied about the money and where it went. This explained why the good suits hadn't found it when they tossed the house and pored over their financial records. Doc assumed that the house had been titled in her in-laws' name, but she didn't appreciate that the good suits were out of her league and would eventually discover it. The house wasn't far, and Doc turned off a blacktop onto a shell road that led to the house. But he stopped well before reaching a driveway. Doc didn't want the Yorktown widow to find out that he had checked out the beach property and learned her secret. He now had the suspicious deaths of two sailors who mysteriously acquired substantial amounts of money and explosives.

The next morning he sat at his newsroom desk with hands locked behind his head and rocked back and forth in his swivel chair. Doc had followed the story as far as he could go without a break, but he was about to get one.

Clausen came in early as well and immediately began flipping through her notebook and typing with a surprising urgency.

"What's going on?"

"Not now, Doc."

"At least give me a hint."

"A bunch of white racists are complaining about black congressmen getting a free ride on a destroyer paid for by taxpayers. They started blocking the D&S gate this morning. That's where I've been. Those people scare me. They hate for hate's sake. Fortunately, cops and base security are keeping them from attacking the congressmen."

"That's the destroyer that Booker served on."

"Yeah. Now hush."

It was the longest of longshots, but Doc decided to take it. He immediately reprocessed the conversation with Harry, pulled out a Tidewater map, and began to search for the destroyer's probable path. Extensive security surrounded the destroyer and submarine piers, with only one guarded gate in and out. The destroyer's course would lead into the bay, well out of range for the transmitter, until the vessel crossed over Hampton Roads Bridge Tunnel. He turned to Clausen. "Don't get pissed off. It's important. What do you know about the destroyer's course?"

"All I know is the skipper is giving them a slow look at the bridge tunnel. There's going to be a bill requesting a name change to the Martin Luther King Causeway. They're trying to sell that idea to Virginia congressmen."

"When do they get underway?"

Clausen checked her watch. "In about 30 minutes."

When Stone arrived soon thereafter Doc followed him into his office and shut the door. "I can't be here for your morning rounds. I'm going to the Hampton Roads Bridge Tunnel."

"Why?"

"Don't have me committed, but it might be that some people are planning to blow up a destroyer with black congressmen on board. Keep in mind that I said might be."

Stone stopped taking off his sport coat and looked up. "Do you have anything solid on that? I mean rock solid. And have you told the cops?"

"No, no, and no. A lot of what I have is on deep background. The cops want to burn me at the stake anyhow. If I call them with this they'll light the fire."

"I don't care. Call the cops immediately."

"And tell them what? That I have a ridiculous story without anything to back it up. I don't know who's behind it and why, but I believe these black congressmen may be the target. It has something to do with them. I need to go. There are always a couple of state troopers at the overlook coffee shop. If I see anything suspicious I'll get them. I'll call you when I know something one way or the other."

Stone looked at him carefully. "You get some cops to go with you, or you stay here. I'm serious. Make the call."

Doc agreed and rushed out of Stone's office. He dialed Boyle' precinct number, but found out that the detective was investigating an armed robbery and unavailable. Doc looked through Stone's window and saw his editor watching him intently. Doc nodded, verifying that he had called a cop, and Stone appeared satisfied.

Doc didn't trust the cops, except for Boyle, and didn't want to attract the good suits. Given his career writing about criminals, some exceptionally violent ones, he kept a souvenir handy from his days with the Marines. When time came for him to rotate out of Vietnam, men in his platoon presented Doc with a Colt 45 handgun inscribed with the unit's name and a thank you symbol in Vietnamese. Doc had it tucked under his car seat in a hidden compartment dug into the stuffing. When he reached his car Doc pulled out the pistol and slid it into the back of his pants beneath his jacket. After paying a toll he drove onto the bridge. Too early in the day for many tourists and rarely used by commuters due to the cost, he had the lane almost to himself. When Doc reached a point where the bridge led into a deep tunnel that allowed large ships to pass over it he pulled into a parking area.

Only one other car had parked there. Looking back toward Norfolk Doc noticed the destroyer closing. He saw a bald, bearded man wearing sunglasses in the driver's seat of the other car looking at what might be a map. Doc walked toward the passenger side of the vehicle to ask if the driver had observed anything suspicious. When Doc leaned into the open window he noticed that the passenger seat had been lowered to an almost flat position. Several things saved his life. A school bus full of children on a field trip was passing the scenic overlook. The killer had not attached his silencer, and gunfire might have led to unacceptable collateral damage. The destroyer was coming in range, and the assassin had been focused on the transmitter when Doc leaned toward the window. Lee grabbed Doc's jacket with one hand and punched him with the other. The killer leaned forward, braced himself with his feet against the car door, and pulled Doc through the window. He then shoved him into the back seat before returning to the transmitter, but it had disappeared during the altercation. Doc appeared to be unconscious, so Lee anxiously searched the floorboard to locate the transmitter.

When he found the device and rose up the killer expected to see a destroyer, but instead saw the barrel of

Doc's gun. Doc warned him. "Drop that thing or I'll blow your head off."

"Can't do that."

"Too bad." Doc fired, and the noise in the enclosed space deafened both of them. Doc had aimed at the man's shoulder to avoid a fatal wound, but his assailant lunged and changed the bullet's trajectory. The round's impact blew Lee backward, and he collapsed. Doc saw blood spurting from a chest wound and tried to slow the bleeding, but Doc's injuries and pain soon overwhelmed him. Deafened by the gunfire and both dizzy and sick, he opened the car door to vomit on the pavement. Doc steadied himself with both hands on the concrete and heard a car pull up beside him. He hoped that troopers from the overlook had come to his rescue, but the two men who exited were wearing suits.

6

Doc woke up groggy about nightfall and saw Boyle in a recliner across the hospital room.

"What are you doing here?" he asked.

"I'm here because people interested in this situation looked for a friend to come talk with you, but they couldn't find anyone. So Mac told them to come see me."

"I have one hell of a headache, my chest hurts bad, and my legs are killing me. Would you please call a nurse? I need something strong."

Boyle nodded toward a milky green metal table beside Doc's bed. "The nurse put some pain meds and a pitcher of water over there. That's all you get."

"No morphine drip?" He shrugged, popped two pills into his mouth, and chased them with water before turning toward Boyle. "Do you know what all is wrong with me?"

"A busted jaw, two cracked ribs, a twisted knee, scraped shins, and a mild concussion."

"How much do you know about what happened?"

"Not much, and that's all I want to know."

"I'm sitting on a big story. A huge story."

"That may be, but I don't want to know about it, and you don't want to know more about it either. Walk away."

"I can't do that."

"You don't have much choice."

"What do you mean?"

Boyle leaned forward, elbows on his knees, with his chin resting on folded hands. "I'm here to convince you that you cannot lift the weight coming down on you if you don't walk away."

"So convince me."

"Let's suppose the good suits got a tip from a retired military demolitions expert, a cop who broke his word. They found you on the bridge and called in some federal narcs, or so they say, who located a lot of cash and cocaine hidden in your car. The gun that killed the guy, whoever he was, has your prints all over it. Another drug deal gone bad, right? Seems like that crime has become a wave these days."

"That's all bullshit."

"Also, suppose that the narcs tossed your house and found more coke and even a joint in a Bible. I told them that if the Bible looked used it couldn't be yours, but you'll own it in their report. They scared your roommate so bad she's headed home to mommy and daddy in Charleston as fast as her beat-up Ford will carry her. And that was all since early this morning. No telling what's on tap for tomorrow."

"More bullshit. The guy I shot planned to blow up that destroyer with black politicians on board. Booker tried to hide front-end money someone gave him to plant the bomb by bragging about gambling winnings, but that was a lie. I figure he got killed before the final payment was delivered. The Yorktown widow knows about the dirty money. She and her husband, who provided the C4, were in a big hurry to spend some of it. The good suits will find it eventually. I have to get out of here and go to the paper."

"I think you'll find out you don't work there anymore. How that came about I don't know. Actually, I don't know how any of this got worked out."

This news stunned Doc. "How do you know all this?"

"The good suits told me most of it. Don't ask me who they are because I don't know. The Chief called me in and told me to listen to what they had to say. Chief left his office so he can't verify anything. The two suits told me their version of events and assured me that an official report would follow as soon as they cleared up some details. I figure you're one of the details."

Doc shook his sore head. "I feel like I'm in a Hitchcock movie."

"Never met the man, but a lawyer in your corporate office contacted me and said a deal had been worked out, and the city editor would explain it to you. Apparently you can shut up and have a job at another paper in their chain. Or you can get collared for possession with intent to sell, manslaughter, and a lot of other stuff they'll tack on. That's the takeaway."

"I may call Monroe and take them on."

"That's a play, but I doubt you'll win. The good suits who talked to me are way out of your league. Mine too. Monroe can't handle them either given his coke habit, activities with underage girls, and offshore accounts. I guarantee you these guys are very good at making problems go away. It's what they do. Think about it. Who wants this story on the street? A rogue sailor, a career man with a high security clearance, tries to blow up his ship with black congressmen on board. You think the Navy wants to read about that in the newspapers? The Pentagon? Who gains by airing that out? These people will handle it their way, internally, the way they always do. In the end their report will be buried so deep that coal miners couldn't find it."

"Can I put you on record if I write a story?"

"Are you going to write it from prison? Besides, you know my wife's driving record and some of the stuff I've done to protect her. They would burn me to the ground. I have kids and a mortgage I can hardly afford. You know that story."

Both men remained silent for a moment or two, pondering the situation. "I cannot believe I'm in this hole," Doc said.

"Well you are. My advice is to stop digging and climb out any way you can."

"So they get away with it. No one does a thing about it."

"I saw a lot of stuff in Nam that was wrong. Bad wrong. But I left it all behind. I had to. You saw the same stuff I did. My point is that neither one of us can do a thing about a lot of bad stuff we know about. You best get out of the way or you'll get run over by the good suits. That's the way it is and always will be." Boyle stood. "The doctor should be in here any minute to check on you, and I said what I came here to say. My advice is to move on." Boyle made that recommendation and walked out.

After the doctor gave him a going over and dire warnings about checking himself out so soon, Doc limped out of the hospital after dark. He took a pound of medical paperwork and a sack full of pain killers with him. He saw his car in a parking place near the emergency room exit, which surprised him since Doc had no idea how it got there. He took slow, small steps to the Datsun, completed a careful drive to the newspaper, and pulled into an almost empty parking lot. When he opened the double glass doors and shuffled into the marble lobby, more difficulties waited there. Two husky security guards confronted him immediately. "Are you Harold Hardesty?" one asked.

"Yes, but I hate that name. You can call me Doc since I assume we'll get to know each other better." The guard demanded that he surrender his press identity card and building pass. Doc recoiled. "All I'm trying to do is get up to the newsroom. I'm not a serial killer, and I don't know why you're hassling me."

The younger of the two stood directly in front of Doc, blocking his path. "I'm asking you nicely to give us your credentials. You're not going anywhere until that happens. If that does not happen I'll call the police and have them pick you up for disorderly conduct and trespass. If you hand over your stuff I'll escort you up to the newsroom to get your personal things. That's the only place in this building you're allowed to go. You have a few minutes up there to get your stuff before I escort you out the building."

Faced with the guard's implacable attitude Doc caved in and slowly followed him up marble stairs to the second floor. That short trip hurt immensely and caused him to be short of breath. Had it not been for the pain meds he couldn't have made the climb without passing out. The expansive newsroom was empty except for two janitors attempting to clean up the detritus of a news deadline. Stone waited for him in his glass-enclosed office.

He opened his office door for Doc, but the security guard interceded. "I was told to let him clean out his desk, that's all."

"I have liability releases to get signed along with other paperwork, his severance check, and I need notes on stories he was working on. So you call the sixth floor lawyers and tell them that you refused to allow him to sign liability releases they're waiting on. Let me know how that works out for your law enforcement career."

The guard pondered this for a moment then said, "Okay, but I'm waiting over there, and he goes with me after he has time to do that. How long will it take?"

"He'll want to read the documents before signing them and resolve any questions he has. So I don't know how long.

Every page is full of lawyer gibberish. I read them twice and still don't understand what they say."

Doc followed Stone into his office and shut the door behind him. They both sat down on opposite sides of the city editor's desk and looked at each other. Stone spoke first. "I didn't know you were hurt that bad. Your face looks awful. What else is wrong?"

"Everything else. I'd like to offer up a country boy witticism, but I can't think of any."

"Good. I'm tired of listening to that crap." Stone handed Doc a stack of papers. "You need to read this stuff or act like you're reading it so Barney doesn't throw down on us."

Doc looked at the first page. "I assume this stack removes any possibility of me ever causing harm or embarrassment to the corporation. Why does it take this much paperwork? They should have used two sentences. 'You're screwed. Sign here if you understand.'"

"Go through those pages like you're actually reading them. Though I had very few chances to help you I did get some things done. As part of the deal you get a six-month severance check. They wanted you to take a gig in Guam, but I convinced the sixth floor to send you to our Memphis paper if you want to go. I know the city editor. He's a good man and a friend. Jack Harrison agreed to put you on a general assignment beat. Plus, all of your legal problems go away, or so I'm told, though I don't know what all those problems are. The sixth floor lawyers at first talked like they had all the big sticks and carrots. I convinced them that you're a coke-fueled wild man and might turn down their offer and sell your story, whatever it is, in New York. If that happens they cannot buy their way out of this mess. I told them they could read all about it in *The New York Times*. Our stalwart publisher started hyperventilating and told the lawyers to shut up. So the deal improved a little. It's not much, but it's all I could get you. I had my personal attorney read the documents, and he says they say what I assumed they would. Sorry, but I could only help you a little."

"Thanks, I need all I can get. How did this situation go down with the other reporters and editors?"

"Except for Clausen they scattered like flushed quail. As you know, Clausen has no runaway in her. I know very little about how it went upstairs. Meetings on the sixth floor mostly had lawyers, a corporate heavy hitter, and people I've never seen before. They only brought me in to announce big decisions and insist that I sell the deal to you. That's when I negotiated. A few hours after I left the meeting they dumped this paperwork on me. Clausen got pissed and tried to start a newsroom revolt. Now she's covering furniture construction in High Point, North Carolina. I figure after you leave town I can bring her back."

"How about our courageous managing editor. Did the M. E. object to anything?"

"As you know, he's too near retirement to start a brawl with the corporation that owns us. In other news a huge man called Tiny came by. He appeared to be out of sorts and wanted to know where you were or the location of your car. I told him that I had no idea about either one."

Doc listened as he turned more pages and continued to act like he was reviewing the documents. "I'm absolutely stunned that so much stuff got fixed so quick. These guys know how to create a smoke screen fast."

"I've the impression that some of it was already in the works. It all seemed too pat to be ad lib, but the unidentified men were ice cold, impossible to read."

"So what happens if I don't go gently into the night?"

"They'll destroy your career and maybe your world."

"We're missing out on the biggest story of our careers. There are powerful people out there who planned to kill those black congressmen. It's a hell of a story."

"Maybe so, but it won't roll off our presses. I don't want to tell you what to do, but I'm inclined to think that orderly withdrawal may be the soundest option. Live to fight another day, or so the cliché goes. At least you can start over with your reputation intact."

Doc thought for a moment. "I appreciate what you've done for me, Carter. I know I'm an editor's worst nightmare."

Stone smiled. "All good reporters are nightmares in one way or another. When I talked to Jack about taking you in Memphis he wanted your story. I gave him some of it, and I also mentioned the many Virginia Press Association awards you've won. He was impressed, and Jack is a hard man to impress." Stone turned toward the newsroom. "By the way, Barney is getting twitchy out there. He may open fire."

After finishing his apparent review of the papers Doc took his editor's advice. He signed three copies, accepted his paycheck, and asked Stone to contact Harrison for a week's delay in his arrival for medical reasons. Stone agreed. As Doc put personal items from his desk into an empty shipping box he noticed that all of his story notes were gone. "What happened to all my notes?"

"Sixth floor lawyers took all of it."

"They don't miss a thing, do they?"

"Not much." After Doc filled the small box his editor put a hand gingerly on his shoulder. "Keep in mind that Jack is a good man. You can trust him. Remember that. It's important. You can trust him with anything. And don't give up. Don't let this change who you are." Doc recognized this message inside a message, but the guard approached, and the moment passed.

Doc's personal property amounted to very little so he could carry his box while slowly following the guard downstairs. But the pain caused him to pause once, and he almost fell. Doc was surprised by the young man's change of tone. "Do you need help carrying that stuff out to your car?"

"No. I can manage, but thanks for asking." Doc's next challenge was the drive to Willoughby Spit without killing any pedestrians or ramming other vehicles. But he drove slow and made it home. There he found another surprise. The front door remained unlocked, and the place had been ransacked. In her effort to depart quickly Karen scattered books and his clothing throughout the four rooms. She took her clothes, cooking utensils, and the Bible, but Doc's two cans of beer remained in the refrigerator. He couldn't recall if the Bible still held a joint, but Doc hoped so. He wanted her preacher father to find it and form a prayer chain to save her soul.

The consequences of pain and pain pills made him drowsy, so he locked the door and laid down on the stripped bed. Doc soon dozed, then fell into a deep sleep that lasted until sunlight pierced the curtains and he heard a knock on the door. At first Doc thought about ignoring it, but decided to find out what else was going wrong. When he opened the door Doc found Clausen holding two cups of coffee. "What are you doing here?"

"I'm not here," she said after handing him a cup and walking in. "I'm in a Carolina factory watching men sand coffee tables. Who beat you up?"

"I didn't catch his name."

"Well he did a good job."

"I agree. I should warn you that being seen with me is not a good career move."

"I know, but I want to find out what happened. You obviously got on somebody's nerves. Who was it and why?"

Doc pointed to a stack of papers. "Somewhere in that pile is a non-disclosure agreement."

"No surprise there. But I've been sitting beside you for a couple of years now and often overheard your phone calls. You'll find a way in and out. You always do. I know you're jammed up and beat up so I'll go away and wait on your call. You got my number, so call me, please."

After that Clausen walked out the door and Doc looked about the cluttered room. Fortunately, given his physical condition, packing didn't require much effort because few personal items remained in the bungalow. He carried those things to his car and then slumped in an easy chair and pondered what if anything he wanted to do before departing Tidewater. Only one thing stood out. He wanted to go to the bridge tunnel overlook where his Virginia journey ended. When Doc pulled up to the spot Lee selected to trigger the bomb he experienced an eerie feeling. Nothing remained of so much. Doc recalled details of the events that began with a sleepy Marine. But they seemed unreal, like memories that did not belong to him. So he drove away, toward a hotel atop Afton Mountain where he usually ended his first day's journey on rare occasions when he returned home.

While drinking his last beer in a motel room high atop the mountain he decided to call his sister Melissa and alert her about his arrival. When she answered the phone Doc heard the sound of many people talking loud in the background. "Melissa, it's Doc."

"Are you okay?

"Yeah. I'm on my way home for a few days. I'll be working at a Memphis paper and wanted a break before starting."

"That's great. You'll be closer to home. If I sound startled it's because I can't remember the last time you called. When I heard your voice I thought something might be wrong."

"Don't worry, I'm okay. It sounds like you have a party going on."

"Yeah. The guys in Gerald's service department are here. We're drinking beer and cooking hot dogs. Actually, we've had too much beer and too few hot dogs."

"I won't keep you. I'll be home late tomorrow afternoon so tell mom and dad. Now go back to your hostess duties."

"I'd rather stay here and talk to you."

"Thanks, but we'll have a few days to catch up when I get there."

While Doc talked to his sister a phone call from Virginia reached the Deacon in Mississippi. The Virginia associate spoke slowly. "It's been a mess out here, but we got everything tied off. I followed your directions and didn't put an end to that reporter, but I don't understand why you want him out there."

"We're having problems with leaks down here, and I need him to lead us to them. That boy can show us the weeds, and when he's finished we'll cut him down too. We have people here who know how to do that."

PART TWO

7

While driving west across the green hills of Tennessee, Doc recalled the last words Lee spoke before he died. During his final 30 seconds of life, as Doc pressed on his chest to reduce the bleeding, Lee warned him. "You'll never stop them."

"Who are they, and where are they?"

"They're everywhere. Don't be in a hurry to find out. They'll come for you in their own time." Lee's breathing slowed and became labored gasps until it stopped with a shudder.

Doc drove slow, enjoying the scenery, since Stone arranged for him to have a week for recovery before reporting to the Memphis paper. He turned north in Memphis for St. Louis and then headed west on I-70. It would take him across Missouri toward Kansas City until he exited the interstate toward Spencer, a small farm community near Joplin. The trip took two days before he pulled into the gravel driveway of his family home, a two-story stone structure north of the small town. Doc's one sibling, Melissa, walked out to meet him.

Melissa Hardin had retained her curly auburn hair, slim figure, and strong presence. When Doc slowly exited the car she saw his swollen face and blanched. "What happened to you? You look awful."

"I feel awful. I was in a motorcycle accident and got banged up."

Melissa walked up to him, then stopped. "I would give you a hug, but you might keel over."

"Let's delay the hug until my ribs heal. The pain meds are helping, but I'm miles away from normal."

Doc looked carefully at his sister. "I wish you weren't so skinny. Why didn't you inherit the fat genes instead of me?"

She pushed back several curls that had fallen down on her face. "I think it has more to do with lifestyle. I go to the gym every day. How 'bout you?"

"I used to go once a year, but I quit. The sweat kept getting in my eyes."

Melissa smiled, put her hand on his shoulder, and gently nudged Doc toward the house. "Come on, let's get it over with. I can see mom staring out the window."

They walked down an old, sun-bleached sidewalk that had partially sunk into the soft earth, past ancient oak trees planted before Doc's father was born. The grass had grown thinner and browner since Doc mowed it when he was a boy.

His mother opened the door, and before she could speak Doc said, "I was in a motorcycle accident, but I'm not hurt bad. It just looks that way."

She grabbed hold of Doc anyhow and hung on for as long as he could endure it. His mother's once curly long hair had become gray and cut short, and she looked a bit frumpy in an apron dotted with flour. "Let's go say hello to your father before I drop the dumplings in the chicken broth."

The bedroom had remained the same for as long as Doc could remember, with faded green wallpaper, maple furniture that retained scars created during decades of use, and the smell of moth balls. Doc's father raised himself as far as he could from the four-poster bed and held out a hand. The effort exposed his white, withered arms in a thin undershirt. "Are you hurt?" he asked.

"Not bad. I was in a wreck."

"Well, you finally made it home. How long has it been?"

"Too long."

Melissa and their mother departed for the kitchen to allow Doc and his father time to visit, but the conversation was one-sided and labored. Despite the stroke his father could still talk, but had little to say. Not much remained of the old man beyond skin and bones.

The chicken and dumplings made a perfect homecoming meal, along with cornbread, new potatoes, and buttered sweet corn shaved from the cob. After finishing, Melissa suggested that she and Doc go outside for a smoke. "Mom, don't mess with the dirty dishes. I'll wash them when I come back in, and Doc can dry them."

"Okay. I'll take a small plate up to your father."

The siblings sat on the stone steps, and Melissa started to light up. "Do you have a joint around here somewhere?" Doc asked.

"No. I quit smoking dope when I grew up."

"That's cold. So give me a cigarette." Doc lit it and said, "Dad is in worse shape than I thought."

"Yeah, he's fading fast, but there's nothing to be done about it. We've been to several doctors and get the same advice. Make him as comfortable as possible. I think mom is resigned to what's coming as much as a person could be after being married to someone for so many years."

Doc took a long drag and exhaled a light gray cloud into the bright blue sky. "I'm a complete ass for not helping you with this. An apology is not near enough, but I'm sorry."

"Nothing you could do. If you're concerned that I'm pissed off about it don't worry, I'm not. Mom's let me carry the load, and I'm okay with that. I don't want to handle this by committee."

"Well, I'm sorry. I'll try to do better."

Melissa looked at the empty barn. Beyond the worn wood fence surrounding the structure stood rows of bright green corn that seemed to go on forever. "It's so odd to see the place deserted like this and to remember it in its heyday. The whole area has changed for the worse. Several of the town's shops have closed. Most of the kids leave as soon as they can. Nobody comes back. If Gerald's dealerships didn't make so much money we'd leave too."

"Are you still teaching the fourth grade?"

"Yeah, but this is my last year. Our kids have grown up, as you know, and I want to spend as much time as possible with them before they leave. We don't need the salary so why not. And by the way, they want to see their war hero, big time journalist uncle."

"I'm none of that."

"So lie about it. They won't know the difference." Melissa hesitated for a moment. "I saw Caroline at the Wynn Dixie and told her you were coming home for a visit. She asked that you call her for a lunch date. Wants to go to Big Burger like you did when the two of you were dating."

"I'd like that. How's she doing?"

"Not so good. Cole's land leveling business is fading fast. Not many farmers around here have money for that now. And he lives way above their means. Cole keeps a country club membership they can't afford so he can play golf with the bigwigs and keep up appearances. Caroline has stayed with him through thick and thin, but mostly thin in the last few years. I think she did it for the two boys. Both are good at sports, but poor students, like their dad. I hope you call her. She seemed anxious about it. Maybe it will cheer her up."

"I will. God, we were in love."

"It's none of my business, but what happened to the two of you?"

"Nam happened. She was supposed to wait for me, but during her last two years in high school Caroline took up with Cole, the football star. She wanted to have some sort of social life. I shouldn't have blamed her for that, but I did. When I came back, in a fit of masculine stupidity, I ignored her and went straight to MU." He paused. "This isn't an excuse, but Nam fucked me up. Had a hard time getting past it."

Melissa noted the pain in his expression and decided to change the subject. "Did you ever write that novel?"

"No, I'm too lazy. Every reporter I know plans to write the great American novel, but they're like me, they haven't gotten around to it. One of the irritating things I've learned from my newspaper reporting is I don't have the talent and patience to write a good one."

Melissa nodded and stared at the fields for a moment. "It's hard to believe how much farming has changed in this area. Few people mess with livestock anymore because it's too expensive, and you can't get the help you need." Melissa hesitated. "The world mom and dad lived in is gone." This observation brought more recollections until they decided to clean up the kitchen.

Doc passed a couple of days helping his mother with minor repairs and visiting neighbors from years long past. The small town had become much smaller since his last visit. It consisted of about 200 yards of storefronts, some closed, along a blacktop main street. While Doc drove down the empty street a strong wind swept it clean. Where once two banks with impressive stone facades served the community, now only one remained. The other bank building became the town's public library. Doc walked in, browsed, and found a lot of cowboy novels stacked on white-washed plywood shelves. A few paperback mysteries looked worn out. The café next door held mostly old men, coffee drinkers who sat at Formica tables bemoaning the corn crop and cost of diesel fuel.

At one end of Main Street customers filled the Big Burger parking lot. Many had ordered at the carry-out window and were waiting in vehicles for arrival of their food. The faded, white cinder block structure remained the town's heart, and perhaps its soul. Kids grew up in cars parked on the gravel. Just beyond the city limit sign at the other end of Main was Gerald's John Deere dealership. It stretched out for about 40 acres filled with high-priced green combines, tractors, and other equipment. Gerald continued successful business practices used by his father. He ran an excellent parts and service department. Farmers who had machinery breakdowns in the field used their C. B. radios to contact a service manager, and help soon arrived.

Doc took his two nephews and niece to Big Burger for a sandwich and milkshake and regaled them with exaggerated stories about several adventures. He cut short his visit home because he couldn't stand the ache of remembering the place as it once was. The day before he planned to leave for Memphis, Doc called Caroline and offered to meet her at the sandwich shop. After she agreed, he mentioned his injuries so as not to surprise her.

He arrived first and took a worn wood booth along the paneled wall. When Caroline walked in Doc noticed that she had gained a few pounds and attempted to hide it with a loosely fitting dress. Still, she had that lovely oval face, blonde hair, and ample figure. After they hugged and sat down both of them looked at each other and smiled awkwardly. Doc spoke first. "Is this a moment or what?"

She smiled. "Yes, it is. I've often thought about what I would say to you if this moment ever came, but now I'm not able to think of anything."

A teenage girl arrived at the table and took their order, two Big Burgers and vanilla milkshakes, the same as always.

"You're the writer. The man with words. So you start."

"Okay, I'll start by saying that you have evolved into a lovely woman."

Caroline blushed. "That's bullshit. I'm fat."

"No, you're not. You're a very attractive lady. Always have been."

She smiled. "Thanks for that. It's sweet." Caroline paused. "I was nervous about seeing you. I thought you might embarrass me by talking about stuff I don't know anything about."

"Not gonna happen. So tell me your story."

"The first part you know. The second part is boring. I'm married to Cole. We have two boys. They'll soon start high school. Mom died two years ago, and dad retired from the meat processing plant. He couldn't make it farming. Now days few people can. Cole is having a tough time of it. I've been cutting hair at Nadine's beauty shop and taking classes at the junior college in Joplin. I'm about to finish an associate degree in accounting." Caroline became visibly uncomfortable. "I don't want to talk about me. Tell me about you."

"Well, when I turned six my mom enrolled me in Vacation Bible School, which I flunked."

She grinned. "Skip to the part where you went into the service."

"Okay, the Navy gave us a test in boot camp to determine what, if anything, we would be good at. The test had pictures of things like screwdrivers and hammers, and you had to check the multiple choice box that described what you used them for."

"I hope you're kidding."

"Not by much. I passed that and another test, and they offered me medic training. I often wondered why I took it. I guess it seemed interesting. Naturally, that put me in the fast lane to Nam and service with the Marine Corps. I spent months there trying to keep wounded Marines alive and pumped up on morphine until evac choppers arrived. It was ugly all the time. Absolutely gruesome." He stopped, having looked back as far as he wanted to see in that direction.

"I'm sorry you had to go through all that, but your mom told me you got medals and that you were a hero."

"There weren't any heroes over there."

After a pause Caroline asked, "When are you leaving?"

"In the morning."

"I was afraid of that, but there's so little left here to see. I want to tell you something, and I don't want you to get mad. I should have waited for you like I promised, but I was afraid you wouldn't keep your promise to me. I was scared and made what I thought was a safe choice. It wasn't. It was a mistake, and I'm sorry. That's all I'll say about it."

Doc nodded, said nothing, and fortunately the burgers and milkshakes arrived. They ate and drank while discussing good moments from their childhood. Both talked until their food was gone, as well as their enthusiasm, and parted with a kiss that suggested desire.

8

While driving down Madison Avenue in Memphis, Doc saw the *Daily Ledger* building on the left. Fortunately, he thought, it doesn't have a sixth floor. So maybe fewer lawyers roam the halls like jackals in search of prey. After Doc entered the small vestibule with wall-to-wall photos an attractive receptionist asked his name and what he wanted. When Doc told her the young woman perked up. "Yes, Jack Harrison told me to take you to the newsroom."

Doc followed her up a flight of stairs to the newsroom. There he saw rows of reporter stations at bland metal desks on bland gray carpet surrounded by bland gray walls. Harrison walked toward him with an outstretched hand. The large man, muscular and square-shouldered, had a flat-top haircut and ruddy face. He had been a tight end at Mississippi State where he earned a journalism degree. "Good to have an MU man on board," Harrison said. "We played your guys once and got our asses kicked. That was the last Big Eight game our athletic director scheduled."

Doc smiled. "What's first on the agenda?"

"You have to go down to personnel and fill out some paperwork to get your credentials. After that I thought we could either relax in my luxurious office and make awkward conversation or go to the Peabody bar and get a beer. What's your preference?"

"The second one." Doc took almost an hour to review paperwork and documents. By the time he finished, the clock hand had clicked to 5 p.m. Doc found Harrison in his small office, and they headed for the Peabody Hotel. The bar took up most of the lobby, with easy chairs and couches spread throughout the cavernous space. Harrison insisted on buying the first round and took a place in line at the bar while Doc admired massive wood beams supporting an elegant ceiling. In the middle of the lobby stood a large fountain with ducks circling in the water, a well-known feature of the historic hotel.

When Harrison returned he handed Doc a glass of beer. "So," the editor said, "where do you want to start?"

"Am I correct in understanding that I'll be a general assignment reporter?"

"Correct. Franchesca Costello is also on general assignments. She's relatively stable for an Italian."

"What will I do first?"

"I want you to analyze in great depth and detail two years of city-county budgets. They are so thick and impenetrable that it will take you months, maybe years, to complete a series." Harrison swallowed a mouthful of beer and belched. "Sorry. I got carried away."

Doc disguised his irritation about this assignment. "Why me? Don't you have a beat reporter for that?"

"I did, but I moved him to features to make room for you."

"Why?"

"The budget project is real, but also cover. Here it gets tricky. Stone says I can trust you, and that's what I'm doing. Besides, if you leak this I can always claim you made it up. It's my word against yours, and given your current relationship with the corporation hierarchy I'll win that one easy. No reporter in his right mind would be envious of your budget assignment and want to poach. Nobody will claim that you're taking too long because they won't know how long is too long. Hand in a news analysis piece every two weeks, and I'll go with it."

"What else is on your mind?"

"Several years ago Stone and I worked on a Jackson, Mississippi, daily. He covered state news, and I had general assignments. One night after deadline we were at Que Sera having a beer and a crawfish po'boy. Something had been weighing heavy on Stone, and I asked him about it. He described a pattern to what was happening to southern black leaders. I told him there was definitely a pattern. Blacks in the South have been abused in all sorts of ways, even lynched for entertainment. Stone said that he meant something organized, coordinated, and sinister. He heard from an elderly black preacher in Greenville about men with dark hearts throughout the South in cahoots, the preacher's description, to eliminate black leaders. Stone believed him."

Doc hesitated, weighing how much to tell Harrison. Then he recalled Stone's parting words and spoke up. "That's the story I was working on in Norfolk. That's what got me sent out here. What did you do about it?"

"We had several long meetings during which Stone laid out the reasons he thought something extraordinary was going on. Stone concentrated on murders having to do with prominent black people who threatened white power throughout the South. He believed that a lot of killings were planned and coordinated by the same people and not random acts of violence. So we began to work on the story."

"Which murders did you look at?"

"Many. I have extensive files at home in my attic. After many months of digging our names popped up on somebody's radar screen---a Yankee troublemaker asking too many questions and his dumb football player buddy. We were beginning to make connections before our M. E. pulled the plug."

Where did it lead you and Stone?"

"Into a shitload of trouble. The Corporation punished us severely. We received promotions to city editor slots at other papers and raises. Both of us took the promotions and signed non-disclosures. But for Stone it will never end, and that's why I'm here and you're here. He's determined to see the story on a page one above the fold without violating his non-disclosure. I have the same goal. Stone believes you've got the balls to somehow get it done."

"So far I've not had much luck."

"I know, but maybe your luck will change. I haven't reviewed the files in several years, but I believe some of the story is already in summaries Stone prepared. He doesn't mention any names of sources. Stone used numbers that are keyed to a master list of names in a binder that I also have in my attic. I can't lay that baby on your doorstep until Stone and I agree you have a story ready to run. I promised him I'd not share it with anybody without his permission."

"What are your other sources in the files?"

"I'm not entirely sure since Stone did most of the work. He had several people leaking things, but never gave me names. Portions of the material became available because of a screw-up. Somebody sent a bunch of their files to a courthouse instead of putting them in a locked room where they were supposed to be stored. Stone found those documents and copied them." Harrison paused when something else popped up. "Keep in mind that the people behind this are devils."

Doc nodded. He knew that already. "One thing I can't figure out is why the Corporation kept me in their chain. Why didn't they just fire me?"

"Yeah. That puzzled me when Stone and I got city editor slots. I don't know for sure, but it may have to do with the fact that they can keep an eye on you this way. If you went to a competitor who ran with the story, corporate fixers would wake up in a nightmare. This way they have you in contractual handcuffs and believe they can control what you're doing. In theory it makes sense. Aside from that, I can't explain it."

"Doesn't it piss you off?"

"It did then, massively, but not much anymore. I don't have the time or inclination to fight them again. I have a good wife and kids, a job I enjoy, and a great life. I'll help you without being obvious. When you get settled in we can move all the files to your place. I'll free up time for you to work on it because I promised Stone I would, but you're mostly on your own." Harrison glanced at his watch and pulled himself out of the leather chair. "I have to get home. I'm helping my wife cook pasta with a red sauce tonight. I'm the sous chef in charge of the pasta, and she does the sauce. Marsha complains if I hold up the line."

Harrison departed, but Doc stayed to finish his beer and watch well-dressed people with cocktails in their hands milling about the large, handsome lobby. After some reflection he decided to follow through with the story Stone started, but he knew that this decision would make his life entirely serious. Doc decided to celebrate his first evening in Memphis by lodging at the Peabody, in its cheapest room.

9

Doc began work the next morning at 8 a.m. Harrison met him at the elevator, accompanied Doc into the newsroom, and yelled, "Hey, everyone stop a minute." This halted the frantic hammering of about a dozen electric typewriters. "All of you need to introduce yourselves when time permits. Doc Hardesty will be on general assignment reviewing city-county budgets for a news analysis series. Help him in any way you can because this is a massive undertaking." Harrison turned to Doc. "Come on and I'll introduce you to reporters in the sports and features departments." After those introductions they returned to the newsroom, and Doc followed Harrison into the city editor's office. Harrison handed him a thick stack of financial materials and pointed to an empty desk. "That's yours. Did you find a place to live yet?"

"I checked the want ads last night and plan to rent an apartment near Overton Square."

"That's a good area. Kind of funky and cool. A couple of good bars and a good café called Paulette's. When you move in let me know, and I'll bring all the files to you. Meanwhile, keep me in the loop."

When Doc dumped the stack of papers on his desk and tested his chair the other reporters began to file by and say hello. One of them, Fran Costello, arrived last and leaned against his desk. She had a pale complexion and long, coal black hair. Costello spoke first. "Clausen and I were in J school together at Chapel Hill."

"And I suppose you've already called her to get the scoop on me."

"Of course."

"What did you scoop?"

"That you left town in a cloud of smoke and flames."

Doc grinned and nodded. "That's about right. Is Clausen back in the newsroom?"

"Yeah. She said the city editor raised hell until the M. E. brought her back."

"That's good for everybody. She's a damn good reporter."

Both hesitated for a moment before Costello continued. "If you want to drop by my place on Saturday night my partner and I will cook you some Memphis-style fried chicken with trimmings."

"Sounds good. What time?"

"About seven."

"Is your partner a reporter?"

"No, she's a history professor at Memphis State."

"Okay," Doc replied, smothering his mild surprise at how open Costello was about a relationship still taboo in the South. When she walked away Doc dialed up a rental company to lease an apartment. It wasn't much. One bedroom, one bathroom, a small living room, tiny kitchen, and barely space for a table and chairs, but it was furnished.

Doc carried in his meager possessions, mostly books, the next day and began to study financial materials Harrison gave him. The project looked imposing, but he could see a way to compare departmental expenditures with recognized standards. However, he would need help.

The second evening Harrison arrived with boxes of materials he and Stone accumulated. After they carried them in, Doc offered Harrison a beer and a chair and posed a question.

"Where's the best place to start?"

"Probably the Mississippi Commission summary that Stone wrote." Harrison pointed. "It's in that box along with documentation."

"I've never heard of that Commission."

"Most people don't know anything about it. But in the mid 50s, prominent politicians formed an East German style organization to spy on reform-minded people and block efforts to improve life for black citizens. Little is known about the organization because people behind it have kept a tight lid on its activities. It's a state crime to reveal anything in its files."

"How did you and Stone find out about it?"

"Stone developed sources that began to leak Commission materials to him, and he found the misfiled stuff. There are boxes of newspaper clippings and files with interview notes and miscellaneous materials. Keep in mind that people interviewed are identified by numbers, but they're reliable or we wouldn't have used them. One problem with the story is that we had to get it right and complete before it ran because our sources would evaporate.

"What do you mean by evaporate?"

"Ask me that when you finish with the files."

After Harrison departed, Doc opened a box labeled Mississippi Commission and began to read Stone's summary. On March 29, 1956, Mississippi's legislature established the Commission. Key targets were people and organizations, including the federal government, that threatened the South's segregated school system. The Commission claimed to be protecting the sovereignty of Mississippi and "sister states," but that was a grandiose ruse. At that point Doc paused. Stone's revelation that the Commission's reach extended beyond Mississippi took Doc in the direction he wanted to go.

The Commission blocked federal involvement in southern states to suppress black civil rights. To accomplish this the legislature granted commissioners extensive investigative powers, even the right to issue subpoenas. The Commission's staff started small, but ballooned into a vast network of spies and enablers. The Commission's power came from prominent supporters and officials. Its investigators gathered negative information for use against enemies of white supremacy. Their efforts mostly remained hidden, tucked away in dossiers, while the organization's public relations campaigns extolled the state's reasonableness in racial practices.

As Doc turned the pages he became appalled that public officials condoned and participated in blatant Constitutional violations. Stone documented how paid informants, including some prominent black citizens, funneled information to private detectives employed by commissioners. The 1964 Civil Rights Act pushed through Congress by President Lyndon Johnson became an important target of the group. The Commission funded organizations established to defeat the act. Stone attached affidavits that confirmed the Commission's illegal activities to prevent black citizens from voting. After Doc reviewed a small portion of materials in the first box he decided to personally interview sources and try to get some on the record.

At 8:45 a.m. the next morning, after Harrison made his rounds of the bullpen, Doc walked into his office. "I have a workable outline for the budget series."

"Good. Try to keep it readable, if that's possible. As to the other matter, what do you think?"

"I think it's massive. When it goes out on the wire, heads will explode throughout the South."

Harrison rubbed his chin. "Just make sure mine isn't one of them."

Costello shared a spacious apartment in Germantown with Camilia Ann Taylor, a black woman, highly intelligent and blunt. After introductions she talked while frying chicken that had been immersed in buttermilk and covered with flour. Costello participated while peeking into an oven baking her scratch biscuits. Doc poured himself a glass of chardonnay and sat at the table to observe the women and provide unsolicited commentary. "You may be the only reporter in the United States who can cook," he said to Costello.

"Wait until you taste the biscuits before you review. And full disclosure, Cam taught me how."

"So how did you learn, Cam?"

"I learned how on a 40-acre cotton farm south of Tupelo. We were sharecroppers, and I have 10 siblings, so I helped mama cook. She was an amazing cook."

Cam was too. She served crispy fried chicken, mashed potatoes smothered in cream gravy with peppered bacon bits, fresh greens, and good scratch biscuits. The banana cream pie had two inches of rich meringue. Doc ate far too much. "I haven't had a meal that good in a long time. I'd like to dive head first into a tub of that gravy."

Cam laughed, and Costello smiled. After they opened a third bottle of wine Doc listened to Cam's description of southern history classes she taught and her participation in civil rights organizations throughout the region.

When Costello took over she displayed a direct, assertive nature that reminded Doc of Clausen. "So how did you end up here?"

"Since you and Clausen are buddies, I assume you know that already."

Costello smiled. "When I called her for an assessment she said gossip was you got thrown under the bus because of a story about racial violence you were about to break. The city editor helped you get this beat. I found out that Stone was your editor. I've heard rumors about why Stone and Harrison got pulled off state beats and separated. Clausen wasn't specific about your story, but suggested its general direction. Put all that together and the puzzle starts taking shape. Cam and I have discussed it, and we want to help you any way we can."

"I appreciate your offer, but you should stay away from whatever you think this is about, and we should change the subject. Cam, I need access to an economist who's practical and willing to talk on background. No disrespect to you, but I'm leery of academics because few of them have street sense. Do you know somebody who'll help me?"

She replied immediately. "The man you want is Hilliard Simmons. He's a black Ph.D. with graduate degrees from Emory. Hilliard is brilliant and knows how to keep his mouth shut."

"Will you ask him for me? I'm drowning in budget categories and numbers that I don't fully understand, but I don't have any money to pay him."

"I'll ask him. I know he can do any work you have, and Hilliard doesn't need the money. I'll see him Tuesday and find out."

Costello used this pause to break in. "That leads me to another question. Why did Stone send a hot shot over here to wade through a sea of budgets unless something else is afoot."

"You can be really irritating," Doc said, "but since you cook good biscuits I'll forgive you. Thanks for dinner. I better go now. Again, the gravy was Michelin grade."

Doc hurried because Helen, the attractive receptionist, was waiting for him at her apartment.

After turning in his first budget story Doc returned to Commission files. They had an ominous warning stamped on them: Persons who "willfully examine, divulge, disseminate, alter, remove, or destroy" files could be fined and imprisoned. That was official punishment, but Doc suspected that the price for betrayal could be much higher.

Materials ranged from ominous to absurd. He found an example of political cynicism in a campaign brochure. A Mississippi Democratic congressman called himself a staunch believer in states rights, the southern way of life, and separation of races. According to him, socialism and communism were spreading rapidly over the world and within America's borders. He accused the Kennedys, a socialist Supreme Court, politicalized federal courts, and power-seizing pressure groups of undermining and destroying the nation's founding principles. The candidate demanded that southerners set aside personal and political ambitions and achieve the South's destiny. Doc found it interesting that the politician insisted in an election brochure that southerners set aside political ambitions.

10

The next week Doc decided to pursue interviews with civil rights advocates who would talk to him. He asked Harrison for a name and phone number of the black Greenville preacher who supported Stone's theory. The Reverend Broadus Miller's daughter Chastity answered the phone when Doc called, and he lied, sort of. "My name is Hardesty, and I'm a reporter at the *Daily Ledger* in Memphis. I'm working on a story about early days of the NAACP, and your father's name has come up in several interviews. I wonder if I might come and talk to him."

"Pawpaw is really sick. I don't know if he'll see you or not."

"Would you please ask him. I'll keep it short and stop when he tells me to."

After several minutes Chastity returned to the phone. "Pawpaw says he'll talk to you Saturday afternoon if you come at four."

"I'll be there."

Chastity gave him directions, and Doc was relieved that his first opportunity seemed to develop without a hitch. During the drive to Greenville he passed numerous unpainted shotgun houses along the road with old cars parked in dirt yards. Occasionally a nice brick rancher with a shiny pickup in the driveway broke the monotony. Often large grain bins and equipment sheds stood behind the houses, and Doc assumed that these spreads belonged to white planters. After following Chastity's directions he pulled into a narrow driveway beside a small white clapboard house.

She opened the door, said hello, and stared at Doc's car. "Would you mind parking your car around back. If some people find out pawpaw is talking to a reporter it might cause trouble."

"Okay," a surprised Doc replied and moved his car.

Chastity waited for him at a wide-open back door. "I'm sorry to put you through that, but better safe than sorry."

"No, don't apologize."

"Pawpaw just woke up. I'm a nurse at the negro clinic, but I'm working nights this week so I keep him during the day."

"Thanks for helping me. Is your grandfather able to talk?"

"Yes, but not for a long stretch. He's got pancreatic cancer."

"I'm sorry to hear that. I'll keep it brief."

As they walked through the living room toward the bedroom Doc noticed that the paneled walls held several pictures of John F. Kennedy and others with Jesus hanging forlornly on a cross. They walked into a small bedroom filled with a hospital bed holding an elderly black man who looked emaciated. Chemotherapy had burned off his hair, and his head looked like dark parchment covering a skull. "Pawpaw, this is Mr. Hardesty. You said he could come talk to you for a while."

The preacher nodded. "I would shake your hand, but I can't manage that anymore. Have a seat."

Doc took a metal chair, and Chastity perched on the end of the bed. "So what all do you want to know? I pretty much know about all of it."

"I'm doing a piece on the NAACP and its impact on civil rights issues down here."

"We've been fightin' kluxers and those like them for a long time. Back in the day, if they knew I was talking to a reporter they'd burn the house down with both of us in it."

"How long have you been active in the civil rights movement?"

"Since I was a young man and called to the ministry. But I didn't speak out loud and clear until the murder of my friend, the Reverend George Lee from Belzoni. A finer man never walked this earth."

"Tell me about him."

"He arranged to have hundreds of negroes registered to vote in Mississippi during the 1950s. My friend helped start the NAACP's local chapter and served as vice president of the Regional Council of Negro Leadership. He became an important man in state voting registration drives. In May 1955, while he was driving home, a car pulled alongside him, and someone fired several shots. They blew off part of his face. His car left the road and hit a house. There were eyewitnesses galore, but the sheriff ruled the whole thing a car wreck. He claimed that shotgun pellets taken from George's head were dental fillings jarred loose by the crash."

The preacher shook his head slowly several times before continuing. "After I contacted the NAACP in New York some northern papers took an interest. But Belzoni telephone operators wouldn't put their calls through to any of us. I went to the sheriff's office and asked for a copy of his report, but they said it was just one sheet of paper since the thing had been ruled a car wreck. The sheriff said the report had been misplaced, but they would try to find it. That was about 15 years ago, and I haven't heard a word since. I'll never be at peace about it."

"When you challenged the cops about your friend's death did anyone threaten you?"

"You might say that. They burned down my church. Then they called all my flock and told them their houses would burn down too if they didn't pick a different pastor. Some stayed with me anyhow, but most didn't. I started doing carpenter work after that, like Joseph. After a few years it all blew over, and I went back to preaching. Wasn't nothing else I could do about George, so the kluxers left me alone."

"Did that end your troubles?"

"Did until I went after them about Clyde Kennard."

"Who is he?"

"He was an army veteran who went to the University of Chicago before coming back here to help his mother with their farm. Clyde joined my church and began to help poor folks who were just trying to get by. I told the boy not to do it, but he tried to enroll at the all-white Mississippi Southern

College. Somebody at the school told commissioners, and they put a target on his back. Cops arrested him for illegal possession of alcohol after they said they found it in his car. Clyde said it wasn't his, and I believed him. They also charged him with stealing $25 worth of chicken feed. He didn't do that either, but the judge gave him seven years in Parchman Prison. He got cancer in there and died in Chicago after they let him out. I went to Parchman and asked for a copy of his medical records . . . " Loud knocking on the front door interrupted Miller, and he turned to his granddaughter. "You better go see who that is."

When Doc turned to Chastity her worried expression concerned him. After she went to the living room, Miller and Doc remained quiet, attempting to understand a muffled conversation between a man at the door and Chastity. When she returned the young woman looked at her grandfather. "That man said he reads water meters and yours is not acting right. He's going to go get a crew and come back so they can see what's wrong."

The old man shook his head slowly. "There's nothing wrong with that meter." He looked at Doc. "Young man, you better be gone from here before they come back."

"I hate to leave the two of you here alone like this."

"I'm dying, and they know it, so they won't bother me. Chastity doesn't mix herself up in these matters so she'll be alright. It's all for show anyhow. They're showing us how it is. Now you better get out of here."

Though incredulous and furious, Doc drove away after his brief interview. When he turned left onto a street that headed out of town a police car began to follow him. Virginia authorities had not returned Doc's pistol so he had no weapon. He drove slowly, carefully, until he passed the city limit sign and the cop car turned around.

When the patrolman returned to his station he dialed the Deacon's number and reported. "Sir, I followed that boy out of town. We didn't cause him any trouble, did like you told us. Do you want us to do anything about that old preacher?"

"No. I hear he's near dead anyhow and can't hurt us. I've got one of our best people keeping an eye on that reporter, and he'll be dealt with when the right time comes. You boys did a good job. I won't forget it."

For several weeks Doc followed the Commission's winding trail of abuse. The files revealed commissioners or their allies tampering with juries, planting evidence, and intimidating protestors. Nothing was out of bounds or too dirty. Doc and Harrison discussed these and related matters over coffee one morning after the budget installment had been filed and sent to the back shop. They sat in the city editor's office with the door closed, and Harrison studied Doc's troubled demeanor. "I see that your reading material has you spiraling into depression."

"We have to nail this story. It's too important not to. And I'm not an idealist, I'm a cynic."

"I think you need a visit to the Harrison madhouse, my home on a weekend. Come by Sunday at noon, and I'll grill some good filets and have the beer cold."

"What time?"

"About 12, give or take."

"I'll be there."

At noon he pulled into the driveway of a neat brick rancher on a quiet residential street. Marsha opened the door, looking a bit harried. "Good to meet you. I've heard a lot about you from Jack, and it's all good. He's with the kids in the backyard making a nuisance of themselves. None of the neighbors have called the cops yet, but it's early."

Doc followed Marsha through the house and beyond a sliding glass door onto a patio, where Harrison's large body was stuffed into a lawn chair while he watched steaks sizzle. Their two children were arguing in the swimming pool. Harrison looked up. "I would try to get up and shake your hand, but the metal arms on this cheap chair squeeze my butt so tight the chair goes with me. It's really embarrassing." Harrison then took a swig of beer. Doc sat down beside him while Marsha returned to the kitchen to prepare side dishes. Harrison continued. "We won't talk shop except for me to ask where you are in the files."

"I'm at the point where white fundamentalists make the Bible agree with their views on segregation."

"Yeah, I remember that. The religious basis for segregation is obvious. If God wanted all people to be the same color he would've made them that way. Hell, even I know that's stupid."

A splash and a scream pulled Harrison's attention from the grill to an above-ground swimming pool. He had installed a water slide into the pool, and his son Jake apparently pulled his sister Christy down the slide too fast. She came up yelling at her brother, and Harrison interceded. "Jake, if you drown your sister it's no more Cardinals games for you. I'll make you watch Ed Sullivan."

Marsha arrived at the table with chips, a bowl of jalapeno cheese dip, and a sharp comment about her husband after taking a seat. She directed it at Doc. "Jack's parenting skills are deeply flawed. I suspect that by the time our kids become teenagers they'll need many years of counseling to achieve a normal life. He's also very little help with my career. I'm a school librarian and have trouble convincing young men to check out books and read them.

Jack's recent recommendation is to stock up on "The Story of O" and "Belle de Jour."

Doc grinned and Harrison popped another beer. "Hey, you asked me for ideas. I guarantee you that'll work."

"Yeah, until I get fired." Marsha turned to Doc. "Now you see how little I have to work with here. I should warn you that Jack thinks medium rare means raw. How do you want your steak cooked?"

"I was hoping for the traditional medium rare."

"Me too. Jack, don't you dare throw two bleeding pieces of meat on our plates. I'm serious. You'll just have to put them back on the rack and cook them some more."

"Okay, I'll give the kids the bleeders after I cover them with ketchup. They'll never know the difference."

The entire afternoon resembled a comedy routine, and it differed dramatically from Doc's encounter that evening. He met his new source, the economics professor, at a small

cafeteria on Poplar Avenue. The materials Simmons prepared were hidden between folds of a newspaper. While they made innocuous conversation over coffee, Doc studied Simmons. He was a small man, about five feet tall, with wise eyes and black hair cut short. The economist sipped a little coffee before leaving his newspaper on their table and exiting the cafeteria.

Doc watched him go, then stared at the whitewashed walls filled with memorabilia about Sun Records. In many photos Sam Phillips, the famous Memphis record producer, stood beside his musical discoveries---Elvis Presley, Johnny Cash, Jerry Lee Lewis, Roy Orbison, Carl Perkins. Between photos the cafeteria owner had mounted dozens of 45s performed by these stars. It piqued Doc's interest because he grew up with many of the songs and drove his parents near crazy when he played them too loud in his room at night.

11

After two weeks of budget analysis Doc returned to Commission files and came upon a collection of reports that agents prepared. He found many instances of intimidation. A successful black businessman owned a trucking operation and rooming house in Philadelphia, Mississippi. Informants warned that he planned to provide lodging for so-called agitators from other states during Freedom Summer 1964. A commissioner indicated to the state Public Service Commission that the man's trucking business compliance should be looked into. Word of this investigation reached the owner, and he got the message. Protesters had to find rooms elsewhere.

On and on it went, one abuse after another. Still, black citizens and white allies pressed ahead despite the costs. The price paid by freedom riders became abundantly clear when Doc came upon a file marked Schwerner, Chaney, and Goodman. He knew a little about the case due to massive coverage in the national press, but had no knowledge of details and a possible connection to the Commission's allies. White New Yorkers Andrew Goodman and Michael Schwerner along with James Chaney, a young black man from Mississippi, disappeared on June 21, 1964. They were murdered in Neshoba County, Mississippi, while investigating a fire at Mount Zion Methodist Church. After Doc reviewed the file he decided that this case had to be backed up by a reliable source. The next afternoon he walked into Harrison's office before quitting time and asked for a favor. "I need to find an FBI agent who worked on the murder of those three boys in Mississippi, someone who'll talk to me on deep background."

"He'll have to be someone who retired or quit. Nobody else will touch that."

"Do you know anyone?"

"No, but I know a federal prosecutor who probably does. I'll call him tonight. Ask me in the morning. By the way, the M. E. is really pleased with your series. He's the only managing editor I've known who enjoys taking calls from pissed off politicians. That means you're getting it right."

"Well, the pot started boiling after the first few stories. I've been surprised by how many phone calls I'm getting from current and former employees about alleged abuses and questionable activities. Almost every day I get at least one letter or call about irregularities."

"Is anyone on the record?"

"No, but I'm working on it. We have to rethink our approach to this series. I want to lead with human interest accounts as a hook for some of the dry material. We can make these stories much more interesting to a general reader."

Harrison nodded. "Okay, but make sure everything is properly sourced because the barbarians will eventually storm the ramparts."

"No problem, but these stories will get more uncomfortable for officials. I hope the M. E. hangs tough."

"He will. Walter's got elephant balls."

Harrison stopped at Doc's desk the next morning and handed him a slip of paper. It contained the phone number of Robert Johnson, a retired FBI agent living in the Heights section of Little Rock. After work Doc called and introduced himself.

"I know who you are. What do you want?" Johnson asked.

"I'm trying to track down information about the Mississippi Commission." Nothing but silence came out of the telephone. "And I need help."

"Yes you do, and you'll have trouble finding any."

"Will you talk to me about it?"

"Not over the telephone. You have to do it at my place with my rules or not at all."

"Agreed."

"You can come on Saturday at three. Notes only. No tape recorder."

Johnson gave him directions to his house in Little Rock and hung up. Doc considered the retired agent's tone and caution and decided that he may have acquired a good source. That Saturday, promptly at three, Doc pulled into the driveway at Johnson's large brick house perched on a slight rise. The handsome, two-story structure had a carefully manicured lawn and a lap pool that ran along the side of the house. Johnson met Doc outside with a firm handshake and led him into an airy veranda. The agent was tall and trim, with a serious face, conservative haircut, and the tan of a frequent golfer.

Doc took a chair offered by Johnson and thanked him. "I appreciate your help."

"First, tell me about yourself. Who you are and where you came from."

Doc assumed that Johnson had thoroughly checked him out, so he decided to reveal everything, scars included. It appeared to work.   `

"Do you want a soft drink?" Johnson asked, "All I have is Coke." Doc said yes, and the agent handed him a can dug out of the cooler on a side table. "Our intermediary told me that you know the meaning of deep background and that your word is good. Are you a man of your word?"

"Yes, you can count on it."

"You've picked a tough nut to crack, but I assume you know that already. I can't speak to current Commission activities, only what happened on my watch."

"Yes, I understand."

"What precisely do you want to know?"

"Why are you talking to me?"

"I'm old-fashioned. I believe the Constitution means what it says and says what it means. Most people you're interested in do not. They think it should be ignored when it interferes with their prejudices. I want them exposed, but I doubt you'll succeed."

"Why not?"

"The Commission is insulated with powerful members dug in deep. I've been told that two of its initial investigators included a retired FBI agent and a former head of the Mississippi Highway Patrol. Taking these people down is a heavy pull. Top to bottom, you're playing first stringers with a substantial budget paid for by taxpayers."

"How did you get involved with this?"

"I was one of the agents sent down here to investigate the death of those three boys during 1964."

"Were you satisfied with that investigation?"

"No. It exposed the sadistic racists that murdered them, but stopped at the Klan's door. The Commission supports violent white supremacist groups. Their agents have informed on thousands of people."

"I found in some material that legislation creating the Commission referenced its mission to protect the sovereignty of Mississippi and 'sister states.' Do you think its influence has spread to other states?"

"Yes. Material gathered by spies comes from other states."

"One document I have indicates that in March 1964 the Commission was already looking into Schwerner's civil rights activities. His death was planned. The other two boys belong in the wrong-place-wrong- time category."

"I'm aware of that."

"Will you summarize what you know about that case?"

"The night they disappeared a deputy sheriff pulled them over for a bogus traffic violation and hauled them to jail. This gave the killers time to organize and coordinate an attack. After the boys left the jail they were stopped on the highway, pulled out of their car, beaten, and shot."

"How did the FBI figure out who did it?"

"Their identities came from an informant, but the files remain confidential. When indictments came down, Sheriff Lawrence Rainey and Chief Deputy Cecil Price were charged. Both had complained about our not including them in the investigation. Seven members of the Klan, including Imperial Wizard Sam Bowers and Price, were found guilty of federal civil rights violations. They received sentences of three to 10 years, but none served more than six years. Rainey avoided conviction. We couldn't try them for murder in a state court because we believed that a white jury would never convict them."

"How did you find the bodies?"

"We investigated the disappearance for weeks and eventually found their remains in an earthen dam only a few miles from the church. That location came from a tip, probably another informant."

Doc stayed almost two hours pumping Johnson about the agent's activities during several investigations, and he ended the interview with a question. "Would you meet with me again at your convenience? I'm trying to digest a lot of material, and new questions pop up all the time."

"Yes, but same rules."

"Agreed," Doc replied and departed.

12

Doc returned to Memphis and stayed at Helen's apartment that night. He didn't learn of Melissa's call until Sunday morning. She left a message that their father died Saturday morning.

Doc called her immediately, and Gerald picked up. "Gerald, this is Doc. Is Melissa there?"

"No, she's with your mom. Both of them are coping, but barely."

"I'm so sorry. I was out of town on an interview and didn't get the message until this morning."

"That's okay. We're taking care of it, but I know they'll want to see you as soon as possible. If you want I can have Scotty fly down there and get you in our plane."

"Thanks, but I'd rather drive. It'll give me time to think."

"I understand. You know I'll help with anything you need. All you have to do is ask."

"I know, and I appreciate that Gerald. I'll be there tonight. Right now I need to call mom's house."

Melissa picked up after two rings and said hello.

"Melissa, it's me. How are you?"

"I'm just about cried out. Thank god for Gerald. He's helping me with everything."

"What happened?"

"Dad just didn't wake up Saturday morning. Apparently he died sometime in the night. Mom fell asleep on the couch downstairs and didn't know it until she took his morning coffee. The ambulance carried his body to the funeral home, and we have to decide on several things. What casket, date and time of the funeral, pallbearers, preacher, and other stuff. Mom is not going to be any help. She's mentally shut down. You need to be prepared for that."

"Don't worry. We'll handle it."

"Mom's asleep, and I don't want to wake her. She's having an awful time, much worse than I thought it would be."

I'll be there tonight. You sound exhausted so get some sleep if you can."

Doc followed this call with one to Harrison's house. Marsha picked up and handed the phone to her husband, dozing in a recliner while waiting for the first football game on television.

"What's up?

"My father died, and I need a few days off to tend to family things."

"I'm so sorry. Take all the time you need. What else can I do?"

"I can't think of anything. I'll call you if I do. Thanks for the offer."

Doc drove out of Memphis in an emotional fog with intermittent tears. He thought about what should have been and what could have been all the way home. When he arrived Doc found Melissa and his mother sitting in the living room in chairs moved close together, and both rose to hug him. They had closed the blinds, which gave the room a dark sense of isolation. After a brief description of what happened his mother departed. "I'll leave the rest to you kids." She walked into a bedroom and shut the door.

"It's been like this for two days. She told me to do whatever I think best. I can't get her to talk about it."

Doc looked at his sister carefully, at her dark eyes and weary expression. "So what do we need to do?"

"I guess the first thing is we need to pick a preacher for the funeral service."

"You better do that. Preachers are nothing but time share salesmen."

"Doc, don't start with the sarcasm. I can't handle it right now."

"Okay, I'm sorry. Does her church have a pastor she likes?"

"Yes, Pastor Rafferty. I don't know much about him. I don't go to the Baptist church anymore. Gerald and I go to the First Methodist church."

They worked their way through the issues---the funeral time and day, a casket, and other matters. Doc took notes to share with his mother, and Melissa slumped in the brown leather easy chair their father preferred when watching television. She looked ragged. "Melissa, why don't you go lay down and get some sleep. You're worn out. I'll handle anything that comes up."

"Okay. I need to rest. I don't know if I'm coming or going. If Gerald calls tell him I'm taking a nap."

"Don't worry. I'll see to everything."

Gerald called, as did many friends and neighbors. Doc hadn't talked to any of them for years and suffered through their detailed updates. He shared as little of his story as possible. While Doc watched them fill pews in the Baptist church before the funeral he realized how predictable they were when the crunch came. During a crisis the locals set aside disagreements and pulled together. In that respect they reminded Doc of Marines he served with in Vietnam. Prior to the sermon he surveyed many flower arrangements in front of the pulpit and found one from Harrison and the entire newsroom. He was surprised to see flowers from Helen as well, but realized she was a lot like the people who filled the wood pews. Behind the pulpit was what Doc and his childhood friends called the tub. In it preachers baptized folks supposedly born again who claimed to have experienced a spiritual rebirth. Doc had been baptized there at his mother's insistence. She feared that he might die and go to Hell without the assurance. However, Doc believed that despite the dunk he might be a goner.

Caroline and her parents sat in a pew near the front that they had occupied for many years. Cole stayed home. After a sermon filled with Ecclesiastes a choir finished the final chorus of "Just As I Am." The congregation walked slowly out and drove to the cemetery for a brief graveside service. Melissa, Doc, and his mother rode home in a black Cadillac the funeral home provided, and Doc saw relief on his sister's face when Gerald pulled up behind them.

They had hardly taken seats at the kitchen table when casserole ladies began to arrive and set up a buffet. Caroline was among them with a large pan of cornbread. When the Baptist women prepared to serve, the preacher waded through two rooms filled with mourners and walked up to Doc's mother. After a prayer he asked her to lead the family through a food line, and they each took small portions. During their meal Caroline watched Doc carefully, aware that he disliked crowds. After he carried his empty plate to the sink she approached him and suggested they go outside for a breather. Doc agreed, and they sat down on a concrete step facing rows of green corn turning tan.

She broke the long silence. "Do you remember when your dad bought that Shetland pony for you? You would ride it into the pasture and try to make it mind you. But it ignored you and trotted back to the barn every time to eat corncobs it found on the ground."

"Yes, and you sat on the fence and laughed at me."

"It was funny. You yelling at that pony, like it understood English."

"That was the most irritating creature I've ever come across, and I have met quite a few."

"You were too much of a softy to use the whip."

"I know, but I can't stand anyone beating an animal. I have never forgiven Gregory Peck for killing that yearling, and I can't watch when Ole Yeller is shot."

They remained quiet for several minutes, watching blue jays swoop among tree limbs chasing sparrows.

Caroline broke the silence. "When I was at the funeral I kept thinking about that wonderful cornbread your mother makes. It was always moist and sweet. We would sneak into the kitchen after your parents went to bed and eat half of it. I got the recipe, but mine has never been as good as hers. I don't know why."

"Looking back, I wonder how mom and dad covered all the bases. They were moving all the time. During the funeral I thought about the fact that I never heard them argue. I'm sure they did, but they somehow kept disagreements to themselves. One would give way to the other, and they moved on. What a remarkable relationship. I think maybe Melissa and Gerald have that kind of marriage."

"I think they do. Everybody that knows them feels that way."

Doc thought for a moment. "Gerald is the only rich man I've known who seems completely unaffected by having all that money."

"I think it was the way his dad raised those boys. The old fashioned country way."

"Yeah, I agree."

Caroline and Doc took turns telling humorous stories about each other to set aside the sadness. Melissa allowed them ample time to reminisce before she came after Doc. "You need to come in now and thank these people. Some are beginning to leave."

Doc obeyed and passed the afternoon talking to people who didn't interest him. His hasty return to the newspaper was made possible by Gerald's assurances that he would tend to things and call regularly with details.

When Doc walked into the newsroom the typewriters stopped clicking, and he took the moment to recognize their kindness. "I'm not a speechmaker, but I want all of you to know how much it means to me that you sent flowers. My family thanks you."

Harrison walked out of his office and motioned for Doc to step in. "Do you need to take more time off?"

"No. My sister's husband is handling all the legal and financial matters."

"Okay, but you just have to ask. The news here is that your last budget story has the local politicians storming the gates with fiery spikes and pitchforks. They demanded to see me, you, and the managing editor. Walter told them to fuck off, or a more polite version of that message. He agreed to meet with them as a courtesy, but we stand behind our stories. He arranged a sit down for Wednesday. Walter had our lawyers look over the copy, and they'll attend the meeting. I figure the corporate boys are doing a happy dance. They're opposed to these allegedly liberal Memphis politicians."

"Am I supposed to be at the meeting?"

"No. The M. E. doesn't want us there. The pols would try to make the story about us instead of them."

"Good. I need to focus on the other story anyhow. I'll try to set up another session with the FBI man. I need a lot of help sorting this stuff out."

13

When Doc walked down the stairs on his lunch break he saw Helen sitting at the reception desk. She walked up to him and put her hand on his shoulder. If a reporter happened by, the gesture could be taken as a simple condolence. "Thanks for the flowers. How did you know where to send them?"

"Fran had me send their arrangement, so I got the address from her." Helen hesitated for a moment. "I wonder if you can come over tonight. I have a rack of ribs from Rendezvous, a pint of baked beans, and two pieces of pecan pie."

"Absolutely. I'll be there."

Helen smiled and looked nervously up the stairs. He could tell she wanted to kiss him, but feared being caught. Doc smiled, patted her hand, and walked out the door.

Doc arrived at Helen's with a fifth of British gin, a bottle of tonic, and a lime. As Helen placed their food on the table she seemed self-conscious. "I should have cooked you something, but I didn't know if you would be up to a visit or not." She took a seat at the table, and they ate in silence until Helen said, "My parents are both still alive, so I can't say I know what you're going through. Was your father sick for a long time?"

"Not exactly what you'd call sick, but after he retired from farming the life drained out of him. He worked hard all his life and became land rich by our region's standards. I missed most of his decline because I was somewhere else doing something else. Ever so often I would hear from him, asking me to come home and take over the farm. I refused, I don't know how many times. Looking back on it I'm not sorry I turned him down, but wish I had handled it better." Doc looked at her soft expression and realized that she cared about him. Then he noticed her sly smile. "What are you thinking?"

"I hear all the newsroom gossip, and you have the reporters bumfuzzled. They were expecting a hard-charger, someone entirely different from who you really are. They don't know what to make of you. Fran is determined to figure you out. She already knows we see each other, but I don't know how she found out. I haven't told anybody."

"Costello is a top tier reporter with remarkable instincts so not much gets past her. It's alright, I don't care who knows." Doc looked around the room filled with antiques. "Your entire apartment has attractive furniture. Where did you get it?"

"They're gifts from my grandmother. When gran moved into the nursing home she wanted me to have it. All her other grandchildren are boys, and they didn't care. Some of their wives did, and that caused a little trouble. But my cousins told them that gran gave all of her stuff to me, in addition to some money, and the case was closed."

Doc poured them another gin and tonic. "Let's go to the bedroom, and you tell me your story. I don't know much about you."

After they crawled under the covers she began. "Well, you know a little. I'm from Jackson, Tennessee. My mom and dad own a country grocery store near there. You know I'm divorced."

"If you're okay with it tell me about that."

"I decided to get a divorce when I was at a drag race in West Memphis."

"What a lead. Now you've got to tell me."

"I came here to attend Memphis State because I thought I wanted to be a school teacher. Leon is a welder at the International Harvester plant. We met at a bar when some friends and I went for a drink after a test. He's good looking, makes good money, and is a good guy. But he is obsessed with drag racing. My grades were okay, but after a year I realized that I didn't want to go to college. I didn't know what I wanted to do, but I didn't want to do that. Leon pushed me to marry him so I did. We bought a small house east of the city, and it has a huge garage where he worked on his racecars. Leon took me to every drag race in the area. At first I didn't mind too much since he was racing, but it got old. Every penny he made went into car parts. On weekends he wasn't racing Leon worked on a car."

"Auto racing is a sport, if you can call it that, that has never interested me," Doc said.

"I know. One night at a strip in West Memphis I was watching cars scream off the line in a cloud of smoke and burning rubber. Then it hit me. Did I want to do this the rest of my life? We for sure couldn't have a child growing up without a father, so I sat down with Leon and gave him a choice. He could have me or the cars, but not both. I realized when I looked at his expression that he didn't have a clue why I felt that way. Anyhow, he chose the cars, and I left with my share of the house equity and one-half of the checking account. After a few weeks he tried to talk me into going back, but we both knew that he couldn't change. Sometime

I want you to tell me more about your life. You haven't told me much. I'd like to hear more."

"I'd rather turn the light off."

"Okay, I'm ready."

The next afternoon Doc was working late when his phone rang. After he picked up the receiver and identified himself Doc heard, "It's Clausen, remember me?"

"Yes, and I can't wait to hear what this is about."

"Good. I'll get right to it. Stone made me a general assignment reporter. My first day on the beat I opened my bottom desk drawer and found some thick files with notes and materials you compiled working on the story that almost got you killed."

"How did that happen? When I cleared out my desk there was nothing in it but some personal items. I assumed the good suits took the rest."

"The only thing I can think of is a secret ally of yours got there first. I'll not speculate about who that might be. Who are the good suits?"

"I don't know who they are so forget I mentioned them."

"Okay then, I have two questions for you. Do I have your permission to use the material?   And, do I have your permission to tell Fran about it?"

"Does it matter what my answer is to those questions?"

"Probably not. We both know that a story this big rarely if ever comes along for a reporter. And it works better if we have all the help we can get. You know Fran. She's game and very good."

"Clausen, you have no idea how powerful the other side is. My advice is to stay away."

"I know, but I can't. You know that."

Doc knew that, but he tried again to discourage her. "Give more thought to the downside before you do anything. You may get hurt bad."

"They came close to killing you, but you didn't drop it. I know what you're doing out there."

"I just gave you my best advice. Please take it." Doc lowered the receiver, knowing that Clausen would ignore his warning.

The following night Doc called his FBI contact. "Are you busy?"

"No, but I will be. What do you want?"

"I need to come see you Saturday if you're available."

"I'm playing golf that morning, but I can meet with you mid-afternoon."

"Good. Is 2:30 okay?"

"Yes."

"See you then."

They met on the veranda again, and Doc vented. "I find it hard to believe that this crap went on anywhere in the country. Will you walk me through any connections between the Commission and other groups with similar goals."

"We believed that the Commission shared membership rolls from civil rights organizations and other material with klansmen and others like them. I believe every southern state and others as well have klan members. Another organization, Councils, also harassed and intimidated civil rights workers. At its peak they may have had about 200 Council chapters and thousands of members."

"I've seen only a few references to Councils so far."

"You'll see more if you dig deeper. The Bureau eventually infiltrated these groups and gathered information from paid informants. We identified many of their snitches, including a prominent black preacher and newspaper publisher. Commission money financed extensive P. R. campaigns depicting Mississippi as a state where races got along well with mutual respect. Any problems were caused by outside agitators and communists."

"I know about the propaganda. I have some of their brochures and press releases in my collection. I call it the Goebbels file."

Johnson smiled. "You want another coke?" Doc said yes, and Johnson grabbed two cans from the cooler and handed one to Doc.

"What I want to report is whether these people and organizations coordinate with those in other states to commit violent acts against black leaders."

"We know groups share information about the NAACP, Congress of Racial Equality, and other civil rights organizations. They encourage attacks on freedom riders. I met a Mississippi State Police sergeant named Burrell Thompson who saw a lot of it. You need to talk to him if he will agree. Thompson belonged to a coalition of southern cops who helped track and harass supposedly subversive elements. He eventually came to regret his association with them."

"Do you think he would talk to me?"

"I can ask. You need to keep in mind that Thompson was a good cop, but a rough piece of work, real rough. I got to know him after investigating some atrocities. We talked over coffee a few times after he became disabled. I believe he has extensive files on the King assassination."

"Will you call him for me?"

"Yes, but he may or may not return my call this month. He's really difficult, beyond eccentric, but I'll try."

14

The wait didn't bother Doc since he had a deadline that week to run another budget story. He received several letters and calls from women who claimed to have been sexually harassed by a purchasing department supervisor. The women complained to the personnel department, but apparently nothing happened. Doc shoehorned these charges into a piece about local government's handling of harassment accusations. He talked by phone with several accusers, but held off questioning city officials until the last minute. That reduced time they needed to circle the wagons and load their guns. When the story ran, city officials huffed and puffed and claimed that they were in the process of investigating these complicated matters but needed more time to assess claims.

Doc became persona non grata at city and county offices and alerted Harrison. "If this gets worse I may need an intern to start my car each morning in case someone planted a bomb under it."

"There's one intern I'd like to be rid of," Harrison admitted. "But his father is on the corporate board, and I need my paycheck too bad to have him disappear in a cloud of smoke."

Doc occasionally made eye contact with Costello and sensed that she knew about the Virginia files. At first he became irritated with Clausen, but soon admitted that he would have done the same thing to advance the story. While Doc organized his next budget story about relatives hired in the parks and recreation department Thompson called and sounded gruff. "You can come talk to me next week, but no photos and don't mention my name to anyone. Is that clear?"

"Absolutely. Give me a time, day, and directions." Thompson did and hung up abruptly.

Doc had his doubts about how helpful Thompson would be, but he drove to Houston for an interview. It turned out to be a good decision. The short, stocky ex-cop had a crew cut and a limp. When Doc offered his hand Thompson shook it with stubby fingers in a tight grasp. "Thanks for agreeing to the interview," Doc said, as Thompson led him to a table in the kitchen of his small, rundown house trailer.

"You'll have to forgive the way this place stinks. The toilet is backed up, and I haven't been able to fix it. I can't get a plumber in here until tomorrow morning."

Doc could smell it and made a mental note not to use the bathroom. "That's okay."

He heard a growl and a dog scratching behind a nearby door, and Thompson said, "My weenie dog is locked up in the bedroom. He's an ankle biter. The little shit is downright mean." Thompson turned to Doc. "I have doubts about this, but we agree that I won't be identified. I don't want to get a damned subpoena. Let me rephrase that. I better not get a damned subpoena or we'll be crossed, and that's not good for you."

"Agreed. Will you start by telling me why you're doing this interview?"

"I got tired of watching investigations go off the rails because of sick-in-the-head white people."

"Would you explain what you mean by that?"

"Freedom riders and other protesters were supported in various ways by America's enemies, particularly the Soviet Union and Cuba. Both had their reasons. It gave the Russians an opportunity to defend their system of oppression by pointing to ours. Castro was pissed off by the Cuban missile crisis and probably still is. He didn't get the missiles the Russians promised, which would have made him a serious player."

"We were finding connections, but needed more time and space to nail them down. Crazy racists kept getting in the way. A good example was a Fair Play for Cuba conference in Havana. A lot of civil rights workers attended the event. Those people weren't bad, they were just naïve and didn't understand that they were being played. Commission propaganda identified them as dangerous communist agents. All of that malarkey was spun by southern segregationists, and it interfered with our investigations."

"Let me stop you for a moment. The best I recall, Lee Harvey Oswald was a supporter of Fair Play for Cuba. Do you think southern segregationists had anything to do with the Kennedy assassination?"

"Not in the way you probably mean it. If you read the justice department report you'll find no direct evidence to support a conspiracy. But the Commission and organizations like it created an atmosphere that matched mean people with guns and targets. Many of us, including Bob Johnson, tried to keep the legitimate investigation on track, but there was too much white noise. That's the name we gave to what was going on all around us. Right in the middle of it all I took a couple of days off to ride in a rodeo outside Galveston and got hurt."

"Was that a hobby?"

"Yeah, and not a good one. I'm originally from Texas, but I married a Mississippi girl whose brother was a state trooper. He got me a job, so we moved there. I liked riding broncs, but I took a bad fall and shattered my hip. Had to walk on crutches for several months. It ended my career in law enforcement, but in some ways it ended before the injury."

"What do you mean?"

"There's an old saying in Texas---don't piss on my boots and tell me it's raining. That's what was happening in the South. Some cops, judges, juries, and politicians were pissing on our boots and calling it rainwater."

"Did all of them belong to the same organizations?"

"Most of 'em. I investigated a lot of attacks on freedom riders and supporters. Some of them got beat half to death. In a bunch of cases local cops never showed up to stop it. No one was prosecuted because witnesses wouldn't testify. I've always tried to be a good cop. I couldn't stand seeing women and children take a beating while cops stood around and watched. I didn't agree with protestors, but I couldn't live with myself if I stood by and did nothing. A few times I told cops to knock it off or they'd have to beat me too. Word got around that I wasn't with 'em, which means I was against 'em. I figured eventually I'd get set up and not have help when I needed it. If cops want you dead you better buy a burial policy. Then I got hurt, and it may have saved my life."

"Do you think cops would have killed you?"

"No, but they might have watched someone else do it. You got to understand that a lot of southern cops hate you know who. They don't always join violent groups with high visibility, but they agree with the members. They don't spout off in front of reporters or feds. They always got a reasonable explanation for why the black man ended up dead. I don't know where or when it stops. Hell, it may go on forever."

"I'm trying to find connections between organizations in one state and violence in others. Do you know of any?"

"It happens all the time. During the Meredith riot in Oxford I pulled over people with California tags who came to attack marshals protecting James Meredith. They had guns, knives, black jacks, and clubs, all sorts of weapons."

Thompson paused, and Doc broke in. "Will you describe what happened at Ole Miss?"

"Yeah, and I'll start by saying that James Meredith is damned lucky to be alive. If it hadn't been for northern reporters and the Kennedy brothers he would've died in a one car wreck on a dark country road. A lot of black leaders have died in the dark down here." Thompson stopped abruptly. "I want a cup of coffee. You want one?"

"I'll have one if you make two," Doc replied and watched Thompson put on coffee and return to the table.

"Mississippi authorities blocked Meredith's admission to all-white Ole Miss using every trick they could pull out of their hats. Finally a federal court said enough is enough and ordered the university to enroll Meredith. Then it hit the fan. When Kennedy sent U. S. marshals to protect Meredith, rabble rousers called for 10,000 volunteers to help overpower the marshals. Councils asked white students to form a human wall to block Meredith's entry. After Kennedy saw the attacks on marshals he sent in army troops, and Meredith registered."

"How long did protests last?"

"They went on for several days. After the state police refused to help protect the town from rioters, Oxford's mayor called on marshals and the guard to patrol the school and town. The governor blamed violence on marshals, but newspapers sided with the feds. I saw it all myself. People in the crowd threw rocks, bottles, pieces of pipe, and acid at them until the marshals used tear gas to push them back. A Mississippi senator said protestors had to win the fight regardless of the cost in human lives. A hate sheet called

"The Rebel Underground" encouraged Ole Miss students to continue their resistance, and it even supported execution of the President."

Doc used this pause for a blunt transition to the King murder. "I'm told you have information about the murder of Dr. King."

"Hang on a minute, the coffee is ready." Thompson poured two cups of coffee and returned to the table. "Do you use sugar or cream?"

"No."

"I'm not sure what I think about the King killing. Ray told so many versions that it's hard to know what's true."

"Johnson tells me you have extensive files about the King assassination and are an expert on the subject."

"Well, some of that's true, and I'll tell you this before you ask. You can't have any of it. First of all, they're not here. I keep those papers somewhere else. Second of all, I'm breaking the law by having some of it so you'll have to take my word for it."

"I'm good with that. Do you think it was a one-man show, or was there a conspiracy?"

"There were a lot of conspiracies in that murder. Some started even before the assassination. Ray got free to stalk

King by breaking out of a prison that was supposed to be airtight. He hid in a crate stuffed with loaves of bread baked at the prison. Ray was covered with bread, so who shut the lid of the crate before it was shipped?"

"After his escape, Ray paid cash for a Ford Mustang. He bought a lot of expensive camera equipment and moved to Puerto Vallarta, Mexico, to take pictures of naked whores that he planned to sell to porn magazines. He moved around a lot. To St. Louis, Birmingham, Toronto, Montreal, and California. After Ray came back to the states he worked for George Wallace's presidential campaign. He shilled for the John Birch Society and National States Rights Party, a segregationist outfit. Ray spent several months in L. A. drinking in bars, taking dance lessons, and getting plastic surgery because he didn't like the shape of his nose. He pissed away a lot of money on silly shit."

"Where did all the money come from?"

"Cops have several theories. Fencing stolen goods, selling dope, robbing banks, but the truth is nobody knows."

"Why did he kill King?"

"My opinion is that he wanted to make a name for himself, and that was a way to do it big. A lot of crime starts with an inferiority complex, a short man who wants to look tall."

"Do you think he had any help planning it?"

"Don't know for sure. He learned to shoot a rifle in the military. He bought one in Birmingham and headed to Memphis when King was scheduled to show up for that march supporting sanitation workers. The press did Ray a favor. They ran pictures of the motel where King was staying, and some photos had his room number in them. That flop house that Ray found made it an easy shot."

Doc interrupted. "So is there any doubt in your mind that Ray pulled the trigger?"

"No, but he got some help in one way or another. The cops missed Ray by only a few minutes after a dispatcher got the description out about his getaway car. From that point on every cop in Memphis was looking for that car and driver. Patrolmen probably would have spotted his Mustang, but someone led them in the wrong direction. A guy on a C. B. radio claimed that he was following the Mustang. He reported locations that led cops away from Ray's escape route. That guy was never identified, but whoever it was helped Ray escape. In my opinion he could never have avoided the army of cops after him without that help."

"I know you won't loan me materials, but would you describe the sources you're holding."

"I got close to 200 newspaper clippings, trial transcripts, copies of internal police reports, a lot of FBI interview notes, and all sorts of stuff that cops copied for me. I could get in a hell of a lot of trouble if someone found out about the stuff I got."

"Why did you gather all of it?"

"I thought I could get somebody to help me write a book about it and make me a shitload of money. You interested?"

"No. I'm just a reporter. If I find someone who's writing a book about it I'll steer them your way. Why do you think Ray left his rifle across the street in plain sight where people found it?"

"Well, he ain't James Bond, is he? Most of the cops I know think he panicked and did something stupid. I agree with that, and it supports my view that he got some help. During his getaway Ray stayed in Canada, Portugal, and London using good fake documents and a bunch of money. When he got caught at the London airport trying to fly to Brussels he had two passports. That's how they caught him. A ticket agent saw the second one and asked to look at it, another stupid mistake by Ray."

"So how did he get the documents?"

"That's my point. Ray was a two-bit thief from a white trash family in Missouri. No way he could manage quality documents like that by himself, but he says he did. Of course, Ray told so many lies I doubt he knows what to believe anymore. Given all of the above it looks to me like he at least had some help with the money, forgeries, and getaway."

"What are the possible sources for the money?"

"A lot of racist organizations openly raised money for his trial expenses. Could be they gave him cash on the front end that we don't know about." Thompson's dog began to bark, and he switched subjects. "Weenie dog sees some squirrels out that window in there. They piss him off." Thompson walked to the door and kicked it several times, and the dog stopped barking.

"For the record, what's the dog's name?"

"His name is J. Edgar Weenie."

Doc laughed, and Thompson grinned. "I know my life is fucked up, but so what, I'm okay with it. And I'm tired. I want to go take a nap on the couch with J. Edgar. I'll give you some cheap advice. I think people like you are missing the big picture. You're like someone looking out the window for an arsonist when the house is on fire. The truth is that a lot of violent white people conspire to torture and kill black folks brave enough to stand up to them. Many stand up anyhow, because down here their life is unbearable. Some scary people make up the Commission, Councils, and Klans all over the South. That's the conspiracy. Don't forget that Hitler didn't kill all those Jews himself. He put in motion a conspiracy that did, and it worked. But it won't work forever here, at least I don't think so."

"Why do you say that?"

"A guy I served with in the state police was an army ranger who landed on Omaha Beach in the first wave. His name is Terrence Smotherman. Terrence said he looked over the side of the landing craft and saw what was happening in front of them. Nazi machine gunners were mowing down our men like a combine cutting wheat. Wave after wave went down, but more of them kept coming. When the ramp went down on his landing craft the rangers jumped in the water and headed toward the beach. All along the tidewater men were moving forward at a steady clip. When some got cut down, others took their place. The Nazis couldn't kill all of 'em fast enough. The South is being invaded too. Freedom riders have been coming down here in waves to support colored folks standing up for themselves. They all know they may get the shit beat out of them or worse, but they're not stopping, and they'll eventually win. The bastards in hoods can't kill all of 'em fast enough."

15

While Doc headed through east Texas the air conditioner began to fail. Steaming humidity blanketed the hot pavement, and the concrete appeared to sweat as much as him. Open windows did little but circulate hot air. Still, the trip was worth it. His interview yielded important information, and Thompson agreed to contact a black man in Jackson who owned a barbecue joint and had useful information. That's the way it went building a story, one link after another.

The following Monday he walked into the newsroom with his next budget story. Thanks to the professor, Doc had data from comparable cities and comparisons with some questionable local line items. Simmons flagged problems and gave the reporter numerous breakdowns for use in his stories. Simmons was cherry picking administration mistakes. That became an agenda for a brief meeting with

Harrison. The city editor motioned for Doc to step into his office before Harrison's bull pen roundup one morning. After he closed the door Harrison said, "The M. E. is catching all kinds of flack because what few things the politicians get right are not included in your pieces."

"How is it news that those people are doing some things correctly that they're being paid to do right?"

"Funny you should say that since it's exactly what I told Walter. However, he wants cover. I thought of this for the next lead. 'Though city and county governments are matching the records of comparable cities in some ways, there are discrepancies in others.' After that you swing the hammer."

"I can work with that."

"Good. Let's do it."

A couple of weeks passed before Percy Oliver called while Doc was watching *Wanted Dead Or Alive* on television.

"A friend tells me you want to taste my ribs."

"Yeah, I hear they're good."

"Next time you're in Jackson you come my way."

"How about Friday afternoon?"

"Can't. I'm covered up all day during the week. Make it Sunday afternoon. After church I come to the café to do my paperwork. The place will be empty. Come about two and we'll talk."

When Doc drove into the café parking lot the smell of barbecue filled the air. The small building was made of rough planks except at the bottom. There it had tin siding with dings, creases, and dents everywhere. It convinced Doc that Oliver's customers might be good judges of barbecue, but they couldn't judge distances. Oliver, a tall, husky man with a big belly spilling over his belt, unlocked the door for Doc. He had a 38 police special stuck in the waistline of his trousers.

"You don't shoot reporters, do you?"

"Only if they try to rob me. A few ignorant boys have tried to stick up the café. That don't last long. I cook my brisket on Sundays. You want a sandwich?"

"Yes. That aroma convinced me."

"You want slaw on it?"

"Please. What do I owe you?"

"Nothing. First one is on the house."

Oliver returned with two sandwiches on wax paper and extra barbecue sauce in a small plastic container. They began to eat at the counter and discuss the fact that both grew up on farms. By the time they finished, Doc's hands were covered in homemade sauce with brown sugar, and he cleaned them with wet wipes. "Those are outstanding. I've never had better."

"Thanks. My barbecue is real popular around here. People come from all over to eat the ribs, but I haven't started cooking them yet. I run out most every day, and my pit man has to cook most nights. He's an elderly gentleman, and I don't know how much longer he can make it." Oliver pondered something for a moment then continued. "I reckon we need to be clear about something. I'm not talking to you unless you guarantee me it's not gonna blow back on me. These people are crazy mean."

"I guarantee you I'll never reveal your identity. Will you start by telling me why you're doing this?"

Oliver shifted his considerable weight on the squeaking stool before answering. "My daddy was principal at one of the negro high schools, and my mama taught English there. They wanted to encourage their seniors to apply at colleges and had a meeting with the NAACP to set up a few small scholarships. They didn't encourage anybody to apply at white colleges. A few days after the meeting city cops pulled my daddy over while he was driving home. The policemen searched his car and found a bottle of whiskey under the seat. Everybody who knows him knows he's never drunk a drop of whiskey in his whole life. They hauled him off to jail, and the school board fired him. After he got fired, cops dropped the charges. The next week police arrested my mother for shoplifting. Cops searched her car and found some silverware from a store. After she got fired they dropped those charges."

Doc watched Oliver become furious as he told the story. "Were the school board members black?"

"Yeah. I saw the board president walk out of our church after Sunday school that week, and I went up to him and asked him why they went along. He told me they didn't want to get arrested for carrying whiskey or shop lifting. Seems someone called board members and told them what the board had to do, or they all would need bail money and a new job. All that because of trying to help educate black kids. I told the board president to never set foot in here again, and that applied to the other members. They haven't been back, but sometimes they send their kids in to get take outs. I serve the kids. Can't blame them for their gutless parents. Anyhow, you want to know why I'm fed up. That's why."

"So what do you know about the Commission, Council, and Klan, and how did you come to know it?"

"We just know about them. What they can do. They don't try to hide. It all works better for them if we know about them. It keeps people scared."

Oliver twirled his glass of ice tea until Doc spoke up. "I've been surprised at how blatant their threats are. So much of what they do is known, but people who should do something about it don't do anything. It shocks me how deep and wide their power stretches."

"Men from a detective agency that works for the Commission come in here a lot to eat. They sit in that corner over there, sometimes two of them and sometimes four. They spend most of their time eating or talking about something they've done to folks in the negro community. I always carry their food to them. Most times I catch bits and pieces of what they're saying when I get near the table. When they're about finished eating I go over and ask if they want a fried peach pie on the house. They most always do. That gives me a chance to hear more, and it keeps me in good with them."

"Our mutual Texas friend said that you once contacted him about something big. Will you tell me about that?"

"About a day or so after Dr. King was assassinated, Commission detectives were in here. They were talking and laughing while I was walking over there. I think I heard one of them say that their man had led Memphis police on a wild goose chase.”

Doc stiffened. “Is that exactly what he said? He said, ‘their man,’ not ‘a man.’ The difference is critical.”

“That’s what I think I heard, but they stopped talking when I handed them their food. That’s been a while back, so I can’t swear to it. I found out later from the newspaper that some man on a C. B. radio kept Memphis cops going in the wrong direction.”

“Percy, that’s a good lead. A very good lead.”

“I thought about hiding a tape recorder somewhere over there, but decided against it. If they found it I’d be the first black man in Mississippi lynched for shop lifting.”

“Please tell me what else you remember about threats.”

“A couple of klansmen came in here after the Civil Rights Act was passed. It prohibited segregation in places serving the general public, including restaurants. They told me to ignore it. I told them it was federal law, and I couldn’t ignore it. They knew I carried a pistol under my apron and had a shotgun under the counter and wouldn’t go down without a fight, so they walked away.”

“I knew they were coming back so I told the mayor and town marshal what I was gonna do. I would seat negro customers at one end of the counter and white folks at the other end and have a few tables set aside for each. That was the way it was gonna be, like it or not. The mayor came by later and said those men wouldn't hurt me or my family or burn down the café. He told them I was a good negro and for them to leave me alone. But it never was about the barbecue. They wanted to break my spirit, make me do what they said. They can't have a black person with spirit. He ain't a good negro."

"Did those thugs ever come back?"

"No. Best thing for a negro down here is to be invisible, so they never see you. If they see you doing okay, they got to stop you. Put you back in your place. Most moneyed white families in town have a negro woman cooking their food, cleaning their house, and seeing after their kids. They drink water from the same faucet, use the same bathroom, and eat at the same table when they're feeding a baby or a child. But they're not supposed to do any of that. May even be against the law. So everybody pretends like they don't see it. The help can't show spirit. It isn't safe to show spirit."

"Did you write any of this down?"

"No. If they found out I'd be dead by morning, maybe my family too. Besides, they always get away with the stuff they do. They hide it somehow."

"That's the way it goes with these people. Where there's fire there's smoke," Doc said.

"I think you got that backwards."

"Not with them."

16

Doc decided to merge what he learned from his sources into summaries that Stone had prepared. As he read Stone's draft Doc noticed an interesting development. It came after the murder of four girls in a Birmingham church bombing. The Commission sponsored public speakers throughout the country to divert attention from the horrific Birmingham murders. Stone connected Commission speakers with allies in other states. Anti-integration newspapers and periodicals spewed out negative publicity about protestors, who they labeled communists.

Some lies spouted by segregationists reached ludicrous levels. During March 1963, three voter registration workers were shot at and one wounded in the neck. The mayor and Greenwood commissioners claimed that the three shot at themselves. Stone included a Voter Education Project list of 64 violent acts and cases of intimidation against black

Mississippians. Churches where protestors held meetings became frequent targets. A Southern Poverty Law Center report claimed that terrorists harmed or destroyed 92 such churches in Mississippi between 1963 and 1966.

Continuous atrocities led to a growing black resistance. Stone made a list of examples. During 1957, armed military veterans in North Carolina banded together for self-defense. Civil rights advocates in Birmingham formed self-defense leagues. During summer 1964, black Mississippi citizens created groups to defend themselves against racist attacks. In Louisiana, Deacons for Defense and Justice patrolled black neighborhoods with weapons and exchanged gunfire with Klan members.

As Doc's story grew longer he began to notice a gray Chevrolet sedan behind him in traffic. This served as an excuse to dial Ronnie Boyle's private, unlisted number. When Boyle picked up Doc opened with, "Hi there. This is your buddy from days gone by."

Boyle recognized his voice and groaned. "I knew my life was going too well. Are you in Tidewater? If you are, I'm moving to Montana with witness protection."

"No. I'm in Memphis, and I have a serious question before we reminisce."

"Let's have it, as long as it doesn't require a plan with my participation."

"How do I find out for sure if someone is following me?"

"The same car every time?"

"Yeah."

"Drive downtown and make three consecutive turns on different streets. If the car is still with you I expect you're being tagged. Have you pissed off more good suits?"

"It may have something to do with the story I'm working on."

"Stop there. I don't want to hear anything about the story you're working on."

"Okay, let's turn to other matters. How's your family?"

"Things are going well. Delores is still in AA, and so far so good. The boys are into slow pitch softball. I'm trying to talk them into not swinging for the fence every pitch and work on placing their hits."

"Did Mac retire?"

"Yeah. Mac is living in a small farmhouse in Suffolk. I'm worried about him. He's power drinking every day. I've tried to meet him for lunch or coffee a few times, but he won't come. Now that he's not on the job Mac thinks he has no reason to wake up in the morning. I'm concerned about Mac, about what comes next for him."

"I hope that turns out better than you suspect. I know you two partnered for a long time."

"Mac broke me in, showed me how to be a good detective. You don't know this, but he was a damn good cop until he couldn't carry the weight anymore." Boyle paused. "Only newspaper gossip I know is about comrade Clausen. She called wanting to set up a meet, but she won't tell me what about so I ignore her. I don't know if I can trust her."

"You can trust her, that's for sure. Whether you want to is another matter."

"Well, I may do a sit down with her. And by the way, a while back the street said Tiny was looking for you. Seems you did a rabbit run owing him money. I'd avoid him if I were you."

"Yeah, technically I owe Keefer. What's he up to these days?"

"He's spit-balling insurance companies on out-of-court settlements for clients supposedly with back problems caused by car wrecks. I figure every chiropractor in Tidewater has his private number."

"What happened to the smoke and fire I left behind?"

"It went poof. One minute all of it was there, and the next minute it was gone. Chief made it clear that I should move on, that he was sure I would have a successful career in the department and helping me was one of his goals. So I'm moving on and looking forward to that successful career he bribed me with."

"What happened to the good suits?"

"Never saw them again, and I don't want to. The prosecutor's office ruled that explosives missing from a military facility made that a federal matter. Booker was linked somehow to an interstate drug ring, so someone else took over that one too."

"What about the dead guy on the tunnel overpass. The one I shot."

"The chief told me that was another drug-related problem for the feds to work. Never heard another word about that."

"Can you believe the power and resources of these people?"

"It's hard to, but there it is. I've never seen anything like it."

"Did the paper run stories about any of it?"

"Only the company line. Nothing about what we know. I hate to admit it, but I owe you an apology."

"Why?"

"When I went to the hospital and talked to you about your predicament, I should have said you did the right thing by taking on those people. It was the right thing to do, but right things don't buy groceries. I just want you to know that I'm sorry I didn't have your back."

Boyle said goodbye, and Doc stirred another gin and tonic. The next time he saw the car behind him Doc took Boyle's advice. After a second turn the car stopped following him. A few days later Doc spotted the Chevrolet again and began his turns. The car stopped following him altogether. After working late a few days later Doc stopped at his favorite bar in Overton Square. Nick's was a small establishment with cold beer on draft and good Reuben sandwiches. He stayed too long, but since his apartment was only three blocks away he didn't worry about a sobriety test. When Doc walked onto the asphalt parking lot a car came tearing out of a parking spot headed his way. Though the alcohol slowed his reaction time the squalling tires jolted his senses, and Doc lunged back onto the sidewalk. At the last moment the car swerved away to miss him. The shock prevented Doc from identifying the car or its license plate number. Since he probably was over the legal limit, Doc didn't call the cops.

An hour after this incident the Deacon's phone rang, and he picked up immediately. "Yes, what have you got for me?"

"We put a scare in him for sure."

"Good. Let's leave it at that. He'll soon drop like a shot dog, but not tonight."

17

Doc passed the next few weeks dealing with city-county budget matters, preparing two lengthy stories with assistance from his economist and complaints from unidentified employees. When he returned to Commission files he found examples of white integration supporters punished by Councils. A white attorney, a graduate of Harvard Law School, supported civil rights activities. Authorities arrested him and charged the man with contributing to the delinquency of a minor, a bogus accusation. The lawyer wisely relocated. By 1963, Councils received more than $150,000 Mississippi tax dollars. Funds from this and other sources gave substantial resources to a national administrator.

The organization monitored racial views of white persons by using door-to-door interviewers. Canvassing with written questionnaires, Council agents created a climate of intimidation. White people who disagreed with their activities chose to remain silent or suggested that they agreed with their goals. As one might expect, Council polling indicated widespread support. They touted these results as validation of their goals and methods. Councils could destroy careers. A member planted with the Georgia attorney general a fake speech by a black professor from Howard University. He supposedly claimed that black men craved white women and would have their way with them if civil rights agitators were successful.

Doc cornered Harrison on a slow news day after deadline, and they had their coffee in the city editor's office with the door shut. "So what's going on?" Harrison asked.

"What do you know about Councils?"

"I know they can be a nasty piece of work. There are a lot of references to them in Commission files."

"There are, but not on the points I'm interested in. Do you have a source that knows more about them?"

"Yeah. Once upon a time there was a newspaper in Greenwood, Mississippi, owned and run by a good newsman. That is the town where Beckwith lived, the guy who murdered Medgar Evers. Dennis Marrett made the mistake of continuing to write editorials condemning violence against black people trying to vote. The Council warned him, but Dennis wouldn't stop. Then his advertisers pulled out. I mean dried up completely, even some who supported him on the down-low. He went under. Now he's writing editorials for the Nashville paper. I see him at seminars occasionally, and he's still pissed off about it. Dennis dug up a lot of material about Councils. I'll call him and give you an introduction if you want."

"I need it. I've found the story veering toward Councils. My problem is that in our leaked files they are mentioned mostly when something about them is connected to the Commission."

"I'll call Dennis and get his okay before I give you his number. I'll tell him in general what you're doing, though officially you're not doing it. Never forget that."

"Thanks," Doc replied and walked to his desk while spilling coffee on the carpet during the trip. He muttered, "Shit," and headed to the break room to get a wet sponge and try to clean up his mess. Costello thought it was funny and laughed out loud.

"Piss off, Costello."

"Go get Helen, she'll clean it up for you."

"Piss off twice, Costello."

Marrett was on vacation when Doc called, and the return call came several days later.

In the interim Clausen called. "We know what you're doing. I talked to Costello and her partner by phone, and we want in. All three of us."

"I will neither confirm nor deny your allegations."

"I'm shipping several files to her and will bring more when I fly out to help organize things. And don't start talking about your chicken shit budget stories, though Costello tells me they're driving the local officials crazy. I told her you're good at driving people crazy."

"Why are you calling me? You and Costello are running with it despite my warning."

"We need your help with what's not in the paperwork. What's in your head. By the way, why did Boyle finally agree to meet with me? He said you called recently, but he couldn't remember a thing the two of you talked about. Worst case of amnesia I've ever encountered."

"Why did Stone put you on general assignment?"

"I'm not exactly sure, but it may be for the same reason you landed on that Memphis desk. The beat has allowed me a lot of time between relatively easy assignments. I had no idea about the connection between Stone and Harrison until Costello told me. That tightens it up a bit. And by the way, when she first called me about you I told her you were a slash and burn reporter. But she says you've developed a warm and fuzzy streak. What's that about?"

"Maybe it's because I'm the one who got slashed and burned in Tidewater."

"Why do you think Boyle told me that you called. Was that a slip?"

"No. Ronnie doesn't slip. He's always sure-footed."

"I want him for a source. How can I make that happen?"

"Do something for him, then ask him for an easy one. The thing with Ronnie is you always have to keep your word. Always, no matter what. Ronnie and I went through the same shitstorm in Nam. He fought with the Marines, and I tried to save the wounded ones. That forms a bond." Doc hesitated for a moment. "On the other matter, you need to stay away from me and what I'm doing. Don't get involved. It's toxic."

"I'm already involved. So are Costello and her partner. We think you might be getting close to showtime."

"Got to go. If you intend to pursue this, be extra careful."

Dennis Marrett called late one night. "Is this Doc?"

"Yes it is, but I'm not a real doctor. It's just a nickname."

"Makes no difference to me. I'm not sick. Sorry about the delay. My wife and I took our boys camping in the Smokey Mountains, and we're still trying to get the ticks and chiggers out of their hair. Every time we go camping I swear I'll never go again, but I do. My weakness is trout fishing. Anyhow, how can I help you?"

"Did Harrison tell you what I'm doing off the books?"

"Enough to know you've picked a hard row to hoe."

"It's turning out that way. I started looking at the Commission, but now Councils are coming up more and more."

"That's because they're part of the same problem. They ran me out of business. Cut off my advertising dollars after I wouldn't stop writing editorials in favor of integration. I had to sell my paper to a Council member for a fraction of what it was worth. You'll find that one of the Council's key objectives is to control newspapers, tv stations, and people who own them. They want to block information about violence against blacks. The theory is that if their newspaper didn't report it, then it never happened."

"When did Councils start up?"

"Supposedly about a dozen prominent white men met in Indianola apparently in the early 1950s and started the organization. It grew into hundreds of Councils throughout the South. I was told by a reliable source that by 1954 more than a third of Mississippi counties had Councils."

"Do they have members in other states?"

"Most likely. The Commission funnels tax dollars to Councils. They've all become an octopus that strangles opposition. Medgar was collecting affidavits, and that got him killed." Doc heard a crash and yelling on the line and wondered what was going on. He heard Marrett shouting, "Goddamnit Cindy, get the dog." After a short silence Marrett returned to the line. "I'm sorry. My son left his half-eaten cheeseburger on a tv tray while he went to the bathroom. Our lab climbed up on the couch and pounced on the burger, but he collapsed the tray trying to get to the French fries. Where were we?"

"Will you tell me about Medgar Evers?"

"The klan had a death list with Medgar's name on it and other people who circulated petitions in favor of black civil rights. Most people know Beckwith murdered Medgar. His fingerprint was on a rifle scope attached to the murder weapon found by cops. They traced the rifle to him. His alibi was dodgy. It should have been an easy one, but two trials ended in hung juries. The prosecutor decided not to waste time and money with a third trial since another white jury would never convict him."

"Beckwith shot Medgar in the back in his driveway one night while Medgar's wife and kids waited for him inside their house. The killing made Beckwith a racist star. Some people asked for his autograph at Klan gatherings. After Beckwith's second hung jury the White Knights, a group that supposedly broke from the Klan because it was too soft, burned crosses all over Mississippi. I can't imagine how the Klan could be considered soft by any measurement. If the Klan put a Number 4 on a person it called for the murder of that man. Schwerner had a Number 4 on him. I figure Medgar did too."

"How did you come up with all of this information?"

"Different sources, some secret, some not. Though it's difficult for an outsider to understand, a lot of this is common knowledge. I got much of it in a Greenwood coffee shop that I visited every day after deadline. I sat at a table with a bunch of locals, and they would talk about all sorts of things related to white power. I grew up here, so they considered me one of them. But I was the crazy kid in class who they thought would agree with them if I paid attention. Since I graduated from Northwestern in Chicago they believed a Yankee education got me confused. I was careful in editorials to direct my criticism toward general behavior, never personal attacks on a specific person or group. Hatred of blacks is in the bloodstream down here, and people don't care who knows it."

"Weren't you afraid?"

"A bit, but I have strong family bona fides. Both of my grandfathers served in the Confederate Army and are considered to be heroes. They died at Shiloh. My father died in a car wreck when I was 12. My uncle is a Baptist preacher at the biggest church in Greenwood, and my mother plays the organ there. The Council asked my uncle and mother to convince me to write editorials about the good relationship between blacks and whites in Mississippi, but I refused. All my relatives were happy to see me go. Some wanted me out of town because I was a troublemaker. Others feared for my life."

"I suppose the biggest mystery is how did these supposedly normal people generate so much hatred?" Doc asked.

"Many are living miserable, unimportant lives. They aren't anybody, and want to be somebody, but don't know how. When they join the Klan they become somebody immediately, somebody to be feared. All of a sudden they're superior to blacks, Jews, Catholics, and immigrants of every nationality. The United Klans of America is an interstate operation so the losers now belong to something big and powerful."

"How do Councils fit in?"

"They move in the same direction. One thing that might interest you is something a friend told me. We graduated from high school together and have stayed close. Steve runs a successful tool and dye shop, and a Council recruited him. He joined, but after a few months begged off. Steve told them he had to devote more time to his family and business."

"We were having a beer one afternoon on his patio, and I asked him what really happened. Steve said he was at a meeting one night with an unidentified bigwig from some group, and the Beckwith fiasco came up. Men were complaining that Beckwith's screw-up caused an uproar and led to a public relations disaster. The bigwig got irritated and said the problem had been solved. Professionals would handle that sort of work now, and a bunch of black politicians were about to make a big splash."

Doc felt his face flush. "Did your friend describe what he meant by that? Who was behind it?"

"No, but Steve said that you could tell by the guy's attitude that it was a big deal. He quit after that."

"Will your friend talk to me off the record?"

"No, and I won't ask him to. That would put him and his family in grave danger."

Knowledge of this and Doc's other interviews caused the Deacon to call Red, one of his key enforcers. "What's going on?" he asked Red.

"I've been trying to teach R. J. how to shoot a Colt magnum. Got some targets behind my barn."

"Having any luck?"

"Not so far. R. J. couldn't hit the water if he fell out of a boat."

The Deacon smiled for a moment. "I think we have to put down our boy. I've learned that he may be bringing in some other reporters. We can't have the problem enlarged. So do what we talked about last time. Do you remember?"

"Yessir, every word."

18

From an adjacent parking lot Cam, or CAT as her Commission contacts identified her, watched two large men carry out boxes from Doc's apartment, which she had described for the Deacon. The possibility of Doc discovering them was remote since she had arranged to meet Costello and Doc at Nick's for a drink and insisted that they go ahead, even if she was running late. Her bonus for information about Doc's trove and interviews brought a substantial check from the Commission's Washington, D. C. law firm.

Added to her other compensation it was turning out to be a good year. Commissioners paid big fees to someone who could advise them about academic challenges to segregation at regional universities and activities among civil rights organizations. She had acquired membership lists from most entities considered to include agitators and passed them to Commission agents. Payments covered her sister's breast cancer treatment, her mother's nursing home costs, and other family necessities.

Cam learned early in life that hard choices require hard people, and growing up in the Delta made her hard as a rock. She knew that Doc would lose all of his work, but it could have turned out much worse. The Deacon at first suggested a violent home invasion and robbery that got Doc out of their hair once and for all. But Cam balked and forcefully refused to go along with anything beyond a burglary. So the Deacon agreed to limit the assignment to a burglary, or so she thought.

After Cam watched the men carry out what she believed to be Doc's last box she waited for them to climb into their pickup and drive off. But instead they walked back into the building. Cam assumed that more boxes had to be carried out, so she decided to sit tight.

While Red and R. J. waited on Doc to come home they rested on a couch with their baseball bats leaning against the wall. They had picked the door lock to get in and relocked it so they would be warned of Doc's arrival.

Just as Red was dozing off a vigorous knocking on the door startled both men. They were expecting Doc, and he should be using his key. After neither one spoke, Cam raised her voice. "Let me in or I'll kick down the door." The men looked at each other, and Red shrugged and opened the door.

Cam noticed that both were holding baseball bats and had no idea what to make of her appearance. She knew exactly what to make of theirs. "I made it clear to the Deacon that this was to be a robbery and nothing more. He agreed. Apparently the two of you didn't get the memo."

"Girl, you better get the hell out of here. We know what we're supposed to do," Red replied.

"You're supposed to leave now. That's what you're supposed to do." Cam's aggressiveness became especially irritating because the two white men were being upbraided by a black woman.

"We're not going until we finish the job. Now you can leave and forget about this, or you can be a problem, and you don't wanna be a problem."

"Okay, let's call the Deacon and sort this out." She moved to the phone and picked up the receiver.

"Who are you calling?" Red asked.

"The Deacon, and we both know who he is." She dialed his unlisted number, and the Deacon picked up immediately. Unfortunately, he assumed that it was Red reporting on their success. "Tell me you put an end to that troublemaker."

"No, they didn't. This is CAT, and I'm standing in the troublemaker's apartment with two large men holding weapons. And before you start trying to talk your way out of this let me establish the following. One, this is not what we agreed to, and we both know it. I was absolutely clear, and you agreed. Two, this means your word is no good, and I can't trust you with some important Virginia paperwork I have. This situation is entirely your fault. Besides, without the materials we now have he can't publish a thing. So which is it, do they leave, or do I?"

The Deacon remained silent, seething. "Listen to me, girl, you need to remember who you're talking to and mind your manners."

"I'm supposed to be talking to an honorable man, a church deacon no less, who gave me his word. That's who I'm talking to, or is that not the case?"

The Deacon needed the paperwork she possessed. And he knew that CAT had stashed with an unidentified attorney a detailed record of her many years of work with the Commission to be delivered to a federal prosecutor should something happen to her. "Hand the phone to the man with red hair," the Deacon said, and she did.

After a minute of assuring the Deacon that they had all of the reporter's material Red hung up the phone and turned to R. J. "Let's go. We got other stuff to do."

Cam followed them down the stairs and watched the men drive away. The confrontation had given her a migraine so she returned to her apartment, contacted Costello at the bar, and cancelled her appearance.

When Doc walked into his apartment at 11 p.m. he looked about the living room and recognized that something was wrong, but at first his brain couldn't process it. The boxes weren't there, and Doc couldn't explain why. He sat down on the couch and stared at the wall where the boxes had been stacked. The fact that someone stole them seemed unlikely since they had no value, except to a group of dangerous people, but they didn't know about them or him. Doc thought about calling the police, but nothing else appeared to be missing. If he told authorities about the materials, Doc would admit to being in possession of illegally obtained documents. He collapsed on the couch and tried to block out the significance of his loss. It was incalculable, and he dreaded telling Harrison. After a few hours of fitful sleep he awoke to shave and shower.

When Doc arrived at the newsroom the city editor had already finished his bullpen roundup. Doc closed the door behind him when he walked into Harrison's office. The editor spoke first. "You look like shit, and I figure your news isn't much better, so let's have it."

"Someone broke into my apartment and took all of our research materials."

Harrison leaned back in his groaning chair, and his expression quieted both of them for a moment. "Have you any idea who dropped the dime on you?"

"No. I guess they were watching me."

"That's what they do. Without the documentation nobody is going to touch that story."

"I know. All that work gone for me, you, and Stone. And they may be able to identify sources and leaks by analyzing the material."

"Yeah, but it's too late to do anything about that now."

Doc slumped down in the chair. "I spent last night on the couch and decided about dawn that I'm a fuck up. Any decent reporter would never have let this happen. He would have secured the material better and had duplicates made."

"Let's skip the self pity. We both know you're a good reporter. I hesitate spouting wisdom gained from my many years playing football, but here's some anyhow. Sometimes in a game you realize the other team is better. They're stronger, faster, and better coached. So you take your ass whipping and shake it off. There's always that next game to worry about."

"I know, but that doesn't make it any less depressing, losing all the work that went into the story."

"Let's put off the wake until we can go to the Peabody and get a beer." After a pause Harrison continued. "I know this hardly matters right now, but it could make your life a little less depressing. A corporate officer called the M. E. yesterday morning praising your ongoing roast of Memphis politicians. Naturally, he described it as a newspaper's responsibility to shine a bright light on elected officials, blah, blah, blah. However, I suspect that it has more to do with the fact that you're tormenting liberals opposed by the Corporation. So they want you to increase the pressure in case it might help with the next election. I told the M. E. that if we want to get this moving faster we need to switch your beat from general assignment to investigative reporter. He was reluctant, but bought it anyway. So congratulations, you are now an investigative reporter making a little more money. And you will be until you write a negative story about one of the Corporation's political allies. You'll then be fired for incompetence, and I'll be assigned to write obits with the interns since I came up with this terrible idea. So take a couple of days off and let me know if you're in or out. As to the other stuff, I need to sleep on it, and so do you."

19

Doc spent most of the afternoon at a coffee bar brooding. He then returned to his apartment and called Melissa. "It's me," he said.

"What's wrong?"

"I screwed up and lost all my work product. Or to be more accurate someone stole it."

"Why?"

"Long story. Some day I'll tell you about it, but not now. I'm too depressed."

"Are they going to fire you?"

"No. They gave me a promotion and a raise."

"Damn, I was hoping they would fire you."

"Thanks for your support."

"I'm buying a newspaper, and I need your help running it."

"You don't know jack shit about the newspaper business. What newspaper?"

"The *Stone County Weekly Cultivator*."

"I thought the Jacksons still own it."

"Pearl is selling it. Andrew had a heart attack."

"When I was in high school I covered sports for the *Cultivator*."

"I know. That's why I'm naming you managing editor."

"Now that's a leap. Junior unpaid sports reporter to managing editor. What's your title?"

"I'm the publisher."

"Have you talked to Gerald about this crazy idea?"

"Yes, and he had his accountants go through the books. They say it's making a little money despite being grossly mismanaged. That will change. All of Gerald's implement dealerships will make major advertising buys. You know his brother Scotty. He owns grain elevators and markets fertilizer and farm chemicals all over the county. Scotty said he'll advertise more. The businesses that compete with

Gerald and Scotty will have to increase their advertising. Gerald's dad Horace, who adores me by the way, called to say he thinks it's a good idea and the county needs a respectable newspaper. He's majority owner of several banks so our credit is blue chip."

"Stop talking so fast. You're jabbering."

"I'm really excited about it, Doc. I have to do this. I tried being a wealthy retiree and member of local high society, and I'm absolutely no good at it. The girls, as they call themselves, hang out at the country club in designer clothes and play golf, or something close to it. I tried to be one of them, but I just can't do it. You know how we grew up, got up early and slopped hogs before our school bus passed by. And by the way, I hired a bookkeeper, a local girl. She graduated with an accounting degree from the junior college. I think you know her."

"That's a bribe. You know damn well what'll happen if you put the two of us under the same roof every day."

"I do, but she and Cole separated and are getting divorced so I don't think it matters."

"What happened to them?"

"What happens to every jock who graduates from high school and isn't good enough to play on Saturdays. The spotlight was turned off, and the pretty girls no longer lined up. High school hotshots have to face the real world wondering what happened. Cole is like a lot of them. He blames everybody but himself. Caroline stuck by him as long as she could. I know that for a fact."

"So where are you getting the money to buy the paper?"

"That's one of the things we need to talk about. Gerald could write a check for the whole thing and not miss the money, but I want us to do it on our own. The corn farmer who rents our ground wants to buy our southwest 40 acres to even up one of his adjoining 40s. He wants it bad and offered me $1,500 per acre. The paper will cost $75,000, and Horace said one of his banks would loan us $15,000 at whatever terms we want. That would still leave the two of us with 600 acres of good ground worth a lot of money. You could live well off your share of the rent if you had to."

Doc interrupted. "Frankly, I don't know what to tell you. I've been offered a good gig despite my screwup."

"Please don't take this as an effort to guilt-trip you, but mom started sinking after dad died. The staff at the assisted living facility have verified it. When he died you made me swear that I would tell you when mom began to let go. Well, she has. Two of her friends at the place are concerned too. You can ask them. Another personal matter is that the guy renting our homestead is letting it go to seed. I cut the rent after he agreed to take better care of the house and grounds, but he didn't keep his word. You could move in, maybe with a close friend, and live there for free."

"You have no shame."

"Hey, this is a negotiation."

Doc hesitated to reply one way or the other. "Let me think about it. This is a major decision, so give me 48 hours. I have that long before replying to the city editor."

"Okay, but Doc, I need your help with all of this. I'm a little scared that I might fail without you."

"I promise I'll seriously consider it and call you."

Costello approached Doc in the newspaper parking lot the next afternoon after he bid farewell to a disappointed Harrison and a teary-eyed Helen. "What the hell is going on? You and Harrison have been huddled behind a closed door all morning, and you look like undertakers. Everybody is wondering what's happening."

"Well, at this point I don't suppose it matters if you know. You and Clausen have figured out most of it anyhow. I've been working on an expose of white racist organizations. Their activities are coordinated and extend throughout the South. My story began in Virginia, and it ends here."

"Why is it ending?"

"Because someone leaked the fact that I was getting close, and bad guys broke into my apartment and stole all my notes and supporting documents."

Costello stepped back. "Who else knew about it?"

"Not many, but apparently I trusted someone I shouldn't have. That's all you need to know. Stay away from these people."

"Clausen and I won't walk away." Costello stepped in front of Doc to block his path. "Will you help?"

"No."

"What are you going to do now?"

"You wouldn't believe it."

Costello drove to her apartment and nursed a glass of pinot noir at the kitchen table while waiting for Cam. After a kiss and sigh, Cam poured a glass of wine and pulled up a chair. They made small talk about supper until Cam asked, "What's Doc up to? I haven't heard anything about his progress lately."

"I don't know," Costello said. She swirled the blood red wine in her glass and began to wonder.

When Doc pulled up to the family home at sunset with his worldly possessions crammed into the Datsun he saw Caroline waiting on the steps with a cold beer and a warm smile.

PART THREE

20

Months later Clausen called. "Doc, I'm in Memphis now."

"What are you doing there?"

"I'm a journalism instructor at Memphis State."

"How did you get that job?"

"The chair of the department interned with Harrison. It's an adjunct position so I earn very little, but I'm stringing for him on the side. I'm staying with Costello, mooching. And to clarify matters, I'm straight."

"What about Cam?"

"She's at Baylor. They split up after you left."

"What demon possessed you to leave the paper?"

"You met him, remember?"

"What the hell, Clausen."

"Moving right along, tell me about your life."

"Full of surprises. I married my childhood sweetheart, Caroline, and we have a baby on the way. I'll be pushing a baby carriage around the mall, which proves God has a sense of humor. My mother is hanging on in a nursing home. I see her once a week. I should go more often, but it's painful."

"So you bought a weekly."

"Yeah. My sister Melissa and I bought the *Stone County Weekly Cultivator*. I'm the managing editor, and she's the publisher. Caroline is the business manager. It's not a bad gig. We make a little money, and I get to work with people I care about. Melissa wants to go daily, which as you know is a big leap. Fortunately she defers to me on that matter. If our growth stays on track we could get there, but it may take a while."

"All things considered was your decision a good one?"

"I think so. Sometimes I miss the rush, but for the most part I'm happy here. What about you? Do you miss it?"

"Yeah. I dreaded telling Carter, but he understands what my goal is. He's been supportive. His connections with Harrison helped a lot. Where do you live?"

"My sister and I are using crop rents to restore our homeplace. It's a beautiful old two-story stone structure surrounded by trees north of town on a blacktop road. Caroline is in charge of renovations. She's patient and practical so it's coming along."

"Would that be a good place for Costello and I to meet you for a conference?"

"You're welcome any time."

"We need some help. Not a lot, but some. We want you to rework your Memphis notes about the Commission, Klan, and Councils. That will save us a lot of time. If you don't want your name in the byline we'll leave it out and provide cover. But I think you deserve a lot of credit since the bulk of the work you own, and you paid a high price for it."

Doc sighed. "You and Costello must have been cloned from the same rock. You're asking for trouble."

"Maybe, but will you handle the Commission section and anything else you can recall? Costello has the Klan, and I'm covering the Council. Your press contact in Nashville loaned me some valuable files after I kept aggravating him and promised to keep him out of it."

"I don't know if I have time to help with it."

"Do you actually edit the paper?"

"No. I hired a woman who's been the copy editor for many years. Maureen knows what she's doing. I do layouts and edit national and international news digests. I added those when we bought the paper. We use freelancers to cover sports. My sister sells ads. God help the businessman who says no to her advertising pitch. She reminds me a lot of you and Costello."

"Can't wait to meet her."

"Well, the two of you come up with a date and let me know."

"Will you do the summaries and send them to us?"

Doc hesitated for a moment. "Reluctantly."

"We're separating the material into background, connections between the three groups, and anything we can find on joint operations. An economist at Memphis State hooked up Costello with a sociologist at Vanderbilt who's an authority on the Klan. We need you to give us what you have on the Commission and its interaction with Councils and Klan. We're developing a strong case about criminal linkage. We want you to sign off on a final draft."

"Where are you storing all of this?"

"In the locked library stacks at Memphis State. We have duplicates at an attorney's office. He's one of Harrison's buddies."

"Sounds like you're being careful. Much more than me."

"Yeah. I know what happened. That's why we're doing it this way."

After Doc locked up the office and began his drive home he saw clouds of smoke and flames from a harvested wheat field. The crop had been combined, but dry, shredded stalks blanketed the earth. The burning material sent smoke skyward, and a breeze pushed it over the blacktop along his path. Don Higgins, a deputy sheriff, flagged him down before Doc reached the place where smoke obscured the highway. Doc rolled down his window. "Hey Don. Got a mess going."

"Yeah. The county passed that ordinance that farmers couldn't use roads as firebreaks. They were supposed to disk strips. But they don't pay a damn bit of attention to it. I guarantee you if we picked up every one of these knuckleheads they'd have the same story. They don't know how the fire got started."

Doc smiled. "Do you mind if I get out and get a picture of you directing traffic?"

"Naw. Take all you want."

Doc took several until the smoke slacked off and people moved on. When he arrived home, Caroline was on the couch, trying not to throw up."

"Anything I can do?"

"No. Some of the smoke's drifting down here, and it's made me sick."

"You want me to get you a wet towel and some eye drops?"

"Please. That might help."

That evening, after Caroline went to bed, Doc began to reassemble his story. It took him several weeks before he mailed summaries to the two reporters. Costello soon called. "First, my congratulations on your upcoming fatherhood. Second, you had this story nailed. The quote about black politicians making a splash and the references to King assassination conspiracies are solid leads."

"I think so, but keep in mind that Percy was fuzzy about whether he heard them say 'a man' or 'their man.' I planned to go with 'a source recalls' attribution with 'their man.'"

"I agree. Clausen and I want to drive out there a week from Wednesday. Okay?"

"That shouldn't be a problem. I'll check with Caroline, and if it is I'll call you back."

"Good. I'll phone you the day before we leave to get directions."

When Doc told Caroline about the imminent arrival of two reporters and the reason they were coming she grew wary. "They're welcome, but I don't understand why they're coming here to talk about a story. Why do they need to talk to you about it?"

"I did a lot of research on it, but I couldn't make it work with what I had."

"So why do they need to talk to you?"

"Background. Besides, it'll be good to see them. They're good people. You'll like them."

Caroline let go at that point, which relieved Doc. His response came close to lying, and both he and Caroline had promised they would never lie to each other.

When Clausen and Costello arrived late in the morning Doc and Caroline walked out to meet them. They greeted Doc with half hugs and Caroline with handshakes. Each had only one bag for a brief stay. They then settled at a wood picnic table in the backyard while Doc handed out cold beer.

Costello smiled at Caroline. "When are you due?"

"In a few weeks. This is my third baby. The first two came on time, so I'm hoping my luck holds."

"I'm from a big Italian family. My mom and dad have given up on me. Fortunately they already have scads of grandkids to spoil."

Clausen broke in. "Doc said you're directing the house restoration. You've done a wonderful job. The entire place is lovely."

"Thanks. I've had a lot of help from local fixer-uppers. It's good to meet both of you. How long can you stay?"

"We're going back tomorrow afternoon. I have to be at the paper day after tomorrow, and Clausen has a class to teach that morning."

Caroline stood. "I know the three of you have stuff to talk about, and I need to go to the paper so I'll leave you to it. I'll bring supper."

Costello got up too. "Let me go get our file before we start." They relocated to the kitchen table, and Costello returned with a stack of papers. "Clausen and I have prepared a rough draft using your material and ours. We've been over it many times, but we want your input before wrapping it up."

"Okay, tell me what you've got."

"We have proof of the Klan's violence against opponents, but we're not sure exactly when we transition to the Tidewater events. I've included examples of klansmen from one state merging with others to commit violent acts. Our preliminary idea is to lead with documented past examples and use them to transition into our new material. One is from Arkansas. Black farmers around Elaine, Arkansas, formed a union to negotiate fair treatment in financial matters. White supremacists came from all over the region to help local planters punish them. They tortured and killed hundreds of poor black people to destroy the union. There are several eyewitness accounts to substantiate what happened."

"Another example was in Louisiana near a town named Mer Rouge. Louisiana klansmen and members in Arkansas established a Louisiana-Arkansas Law and Order League, a front. They used whippings, torture, and lynchings on both sides of the state line. The Louisiana governor complained that both Arkansas and Texas klansmen were crossing state boundaries to commit atrocities. They then went back to their home state to take advantage of officials who protected them, probably Klan members as well. That's two examples, and there are others."

Costello went for a glass of water, and Clausen took over. "Council chapters are all over the South. They've probably become the country's leading segregation organization. The Commission helps fund them with public money. Councils are strong and vocal in their opposition to integrated schools. That's why they're so popular. Most white people in the South agree with them. A lot of people at first thought they were a good thing for their communities, but then extremists took over."

"An interesting sidebar is that Councils concentrate on owning news sources or controlling them. We know about some of them. People who refuse to buckle are destroyed, like our Nashville source. Another example is a Mississippi newspaper editor named Hazel Brannon Smith. A stacked jury found her guilty of libel against a county sheriff because of her story about him shooting a black man. Council members couldn't shut her up so they started a competing newspaper to force her out."

"What about violent acts?" Doc asked.

Hard to expose with them. The NAACP believes Councils were behind the murder of Reverend Lee who you mentioned. But I get the impression that members are careful about maintaining their image as patriotic spokesmen for communities."

"I think you have enough background sources already," Doc said. "Including documented cases like these will give the piece a sharper edge."

"What are we going to do about attributing quotes to your sources?" Costello asked Doc.

"Don't know for sure. The three of us have to work it out. I can't tie a barbecue joint owner to the Martin Luther King quote, and we have to use it. Percy would be the obvious source, and it would put him in grave danger. I had some interview notes at the office so I could work on them there. Due to that stroke of luck the robbers didn't come up with any of that material. I've thought a lot about Percy and still don't have an answer. The two of you need to give me ideas. Johnson and Thompson I'm not worried about. We can go with 'law enforcement sources.' The pastor with cancer died. We'll have to work on the 'big splash' quote. Don't know how yet."

Caroline returned home after work with a bag of Big Burgers, fries, and milkshakes. Doc and the reporters rearranged their paperwork scattered around the kitchen table to make room for their food. "God, does that smell good," Costello said.

"I fell in love with Doc while having a Big Burger when we were kids," Caroline replied.

"I may skip the burger then," Clausen said.

The women laughed. Doc didn't. "You still haven't forgiven me for rejecting you," he said to Clausen.

She smiled. "Do you really want me to go into your Tidewater dating practices in front of your wife?"

Doc paused, with burger in hand. "Come to think of it, no."

Supper and conversation stretched for an hour or so until Caroline went to take a long, warm bath.

Costello spoke to Doc after she heard Caroline running bath water. "She's a great woman. You're fortunate."

"I know. Caroline is my guide in the real world."

Their meeting stretched well into the night as they resolved issues. After Doc finished reviewing the story he signaled a conclusion. "You have it right. I say you because I've promised Caroline that my past stays in the past."

Costello nodded, as did Clausen, who said, "We've talked about it and agree that given your situation and history you should remain a source. You've done more than your share already. Is that okay with you?"

"Yes. That's the way I want it."

Both reporters left the next morning, and he hated to see them go.

Costello called two days later with bad news. "Harrison told me last night that corporate sources are trying to block publication of the story. They've warned TV and radio outlets that a few radical reporters are preparing an inaccurate, libelous piece attacking the South and its people. No reputable publication should run the story. Corporate lawyers have warned that they will attack anyone who runs it. They're scaring off everyone who owns media."

"They're also slow walking you until they can make it go away," Doc replied. "That's their style. What you need to do is quickly find a publisher. Put it on the wires, AP, UPI, and major papers in New York, Chicago, and L. A."

"I don't know who we can get immediately after all their threats and negative reports," Costello said.

Doc hesitated before saying, "Well, I'll think of something."

That evening Doc held a long editorial conference with Melissa and Caroline in their small newsroom. He laid out the history of the story and his role in it.

Melissa interrupted when Doc spoke about the bridge tunnel confrontation. "Are you telling me these people tried to kill you?"

"Yes."

"Is that why you showed up here all beat up?"

"Yes."

"Why didn't you tell us what happened?"

"I didn't want to drag you into this mess."

"Excuse me! You're my brother. I go where you go."

"Me too," Caroline said.

"Let me give it some thought and come up with a plan," Doc said.

Caroline's bravado was brief. While Doc drove them home she spoke her mind. "Why are you messing around with people who can get you killed? And don't give me some highfalutin' answer about principles. I'm pregnant with our child, and right now I can't afford principles. What were you thinking? You told me that part of your life is over. Then all of this comes up."

Caroline was about to cry, so Doc pulled over and weighed what she said. He watched her wipe away tears and then responded. "You're right. I should have told you the whole story and kept my promise. I don't know why I stayed involved. Maybe it's pride or a desire for revenge after what they've done to me. I can't give you a definitive answer because I don't have one. I'll run the story for them and walk away."

The following Friday, as Doc, Melissa, and Caroline watched, their small press cranked out an *Extra Edition of the Stone County Weekly Cultivator*. Melissa supported

Doc's decision, but with serious reservations. They decided not to send copies to subscribers in order to avoid questions. Instead, it would only travel over wires to major news outlets.

For two days Doc ducked phone queries from other reporters. Then Harrison called, and he skipped a hello. "Doc, I've got some bad news. Really bad."

"What is it?"

"Clausen and Costello were killed last night in a so-called home invasion at Costello's condo. They were beaten to death during what cops say was a robbery gone bad. The burglars took money, jewelry, watches, and pawnable stuff." Harrison paused after his voice cracked.

Doc spoke despite his shock. "Those weren't burglars."

"We both know that. Your name wasn't on the byline, but I'm concerned that they may visit you."

"If they do I'll be ready. Thanks for calling, but I need some quiet time to get my thoughts together." For several hours Doc sat at the picnic table and summoned memories with the two reporters. When Doc heard Caroline pull into the driveway he walked into the house to tell her.

Later that day the Deacon took a call from an irritated corporate board member in Jackson. "Deacon, we think it's time for you to come see us. The Board wants you to explain how this happened, including the deaths of those two reporters. We're very unhappy."

"Those reporters were troublemakers, and my people in Memphis assure me that it will be an unsolved robbery. I believe we have to show these agitators the cost of interference."

The Board member interrupted. "We want to make it absolutely clear that nothing else be done to give the story legs. Our public relations department is working overtime to repair the damage. I personally took a call from our Kansas City associate, an attorney and state senator, who is livid. He was appalled to hear about the murder of those two reporters. He's a member of a large Missouri family with connections to that paper. Those people are enormously wealthy, politically powerful, and not to be trifled with. He made it abundantly clear that nothing must happen to anyone in that family or people connected to them. Absolutely nothing. I assured him of that. The Board has decided that we'll handle these matters from now on. We'll explain how things will work in the future."

A call from Gerald's cousin Theo in Kansas City came later that afternoon. They had been close since childhood. Gerald served as his campaign manager during a successful campaign for the state senate. The Governor's office was next on their agenda. After pleasantries Theo explained the situation to Gerald and made it clear that all issues had been resolved. The conversation ended after an agreement to play golf the following weekend.

The next day Melissa arrived with Big Burgers and fries to have supper with Doc and Caroline. In the middle of their meal she broke the silence. "I first want to say how sorry I am about your two friends. We only met that one time, but I liked them a lot. I hope the cops catch who did it."

"I've been praying for them every day, that they rest in peace," Caroline said.

Overcome with sadness, Doc said nothing, so Melissa spoke up. "Okay, let's lay our cards on the table. Gerald said that his cousin Theo called him to discuss some things, and events surrounding publication of the story came up. I don't know all that was said and why it was said, but Gerald told me that nothing else will happen about any of it. It's over as far as the family is concerned. Theo assured him of that. Gerald was a bit cryptic, but I didn't ask any questions. I'm satisfied that we can move on with our lives, and I can spoil my soon-to-arrive godchild."

"Is Gerald pissed off at me?" Doc asked.

"No. I told him all about it and the history behind it. Gerald said that you and I own the paper, and he doesn't. It was entirely our decision. If I had to guess I'd say Gerald would prefer that in the future we focus on tractor pulls at the county fair and Little League baseball."

"That's good advice," Doc replied. "Tell Gerald I'll take it."

"What I can't figure out is why we haven't heard anything about the story from other news sources. If it was that big a deal, why has nothing else happened?" Melissa asked.

"Because people on the other side have managed to destroy the credibility of our reporters. The whole thing would have to be reworked, every detail checked out, re-sourced, which probably would take forever and a day. And the story broke in a country weekly. That doesn't help its credibility. The simple truth is the bad guys won again."

"That means Annie and Fran died for nothing," Caroline said.

"Caroline, a lot of good people have died for nothing at the hands of the sick bastards behind this." Doc paused. "Frankly, I'm tired of the whole thing. I want a new normal, a peaceful one."

Doc got his wish. He covered mundane farm news, and their healthy baby arrived when expected. One pleasant spring afternoon Doc and Caroline sat on the back steps of their home sipping wine and watching the sunset. They did that almost every day now with Caroline holding their baby boy on her lap. It gave them peace.

"It all seems so strange now," she said. "Think about how many times since we were kids we've come out here and shared our dreams. When I think about what's happened I can hardly believe it."

"I know," Doc replied. "Life happened while we were dreaming."

About the Author

Van Hawkins grew up in a farming family in the Missouri Bootheel. He has a degree in literature from the University of Missouri, as well as master's degrees in pastoral counseling from Loyola University in New Orleans, and heritage studies from Arkansas State University.

Van has worked as a newspaper reporter and editor and as an entertainment magazine feature writer. His books are written for general audiences on topics related to southern history. Van and his wife, Ruth, reside in Jonesboro, Arkansas.